THE MAN WHO (THOUGHT HE) LOOKED

LIKE ROBERT TAYLOR

Other Books by Bienvenido N. Santos:

Novels:
The Volcano
Villa Magdalena
The Praying Man (Won the 1982 "X" Award; finalist for Fiction, English
Division, in the 1982 Gintong Aklat competition)

Short Story Collections:
You Lovely People
Brother My Brother
The Day the Dancers Came
Scent of Apples (U.S. American Book Award, 1980)

Poetry:
The Wounded Stag

The Praying Man was published in book form by New Day Publishers in 1982; it was originally serialized in SOLIDARITY from May 1971 to February 1972.

THE MAN WHO (THOUGHT HE)

LOOKED LIKE ROBERT TAYLOR

A Novel

by

BIENVENIDO N. SANTOS

Quezon City
1983

Cover Design: J. Elizalde Navarro

Back Cover Photo: David Briscoe, Jr.

First Impression, 1983
Second Impression, 1985
Third Impression, 2000

ISBN 971-10-0097-0 (BP)

For Victoria, M.K.

Portions of this novel have been published as excerpts and as short fiction in magazines printed in the Philippines and abroad.

— *Philippine Consulate. . .*

— *Hello! What time it is now*
in the Philippines?

— *Oh. . . Let me see. . . I'll*
connect you to the Office of. . .

— *What you say, Miss?*

$\mathcal{U}$

$\mathcal{S}$unday, June 8, 1969, Robert Taylor died in Hollywood of lung cancer. The news of his death must have been on the late news program on radio and television, but it was not until the next morning that Solomon King learned about it. He was already in the stockyard office, changing into his work suit.

He himself had not been well. That Sunday, he felt the pain before supper. It was so severe he could not eat. It persisted even after two Darvon pills. He tried to distract his mind by watching TV, but it did not work this time. Feeling drowsy, he went to bed, hoping he could sleep. As he lay down, a pinching and scraping of the meat of his arms seemed to travel along the back of his neck, shooting sharp darts of pain in the head and in the chest, and stayed there till he could barely breathe. The pain lay deep in every part of his body and he could hear the throbbing grow, repeated on a spot in his cheek under the right eye, beneath his ribs, behind the ears, in all his joints until there was simultaneous thumping like many bursting hearts, each with a life and an ache of its own. He moaned as he reached for the bottles of pain killers on the commode near his bed. Somehow he must have fallen asleep because he had dreams of home back in the

Philippines with friends and loved ones he had known in boyhood. In the dream he was young and healthy. When he woke up in the morning he thought he would not be able to go to work, but he felt good after a shower and a cup of coffee. He had hurried through his breakfast because that time of the day in Chicago traffic always slowed him down. He had not bothered to read the papers until he was about to begin work.

He had a small air-conditioned office on a mezzanine not far from the rotating beaters on the ground floor. Through the glass panels he could see all the operations going on without the noise and the smell. Sometimes a door stood ajar in the building and the odor from the yards drifted in, heavy with the stink of meat and hides and the offal from Bubbly Creek that wove through the yards, sluggish with sewage, boiling and bubbling as the gases formed by the decayed matter broke on the surface. As a ranking supervisor, he occupied the office all by himself. An intercom and a phone on his desk put him in touch with the boss and other section chiefs.

So. Robert Taylor was dead.

Sol's first impulse was to press the intercom button and tell the boss he wanted to take the day off. He had not fully recovered from last night's attack, one of the worst he had experienced in years. He still felt bad. The office was cold like an icebox. He glanced at the thermostat, but could not read what the temperature was. Removing his glasses, he wiped the lenses and sat down. As he put them on again, he stared at the headline: ROBERT TAYLOR DIES OF CANCER. As he read, his eyes kept going to the photos, one, of the actor "As a Rising Star in 1936" and the other "As TV Actor in 1967." There were other pictures on page two. It was a long story. The lead paragraph read:

Hollywood, Calif. (AP) — Veteran movie actor Robert Taylor, leading man for some of the screen's most glamorous actresses, died Sunday after a long battle with lung cancer. He was 57.

He died at 10:30 a.m. at St. John's Hospital in nearby Santa Monica. With him were his physician and his wife, actress Ursula Thiess, who had spent the night there.

Taylor, billed as "the man with the perfect profile," starred in more than 70 movies and set a Hollywood record with his 27 years at one studio.

There was little in the news item which summarized his life

3

and career that Sol did not know. He had followed Bob's life story on and off screen since he saw him in "Magnificent Obsession" in the Philippines in the middle thirties. He thought, till now, they were the same age. So, he was five years older than Bob.

He was shivering and yet he felt hot, feverish. He pressed the button and the static cut into his skin like blades. He passed his palms over his arms. He felt he was suffocating.

"Is the boss in?" he asked, swallowing hard, as soon as he heard a girl's voice acknowledge his signal. The girl's answer was drowned in the static. When he finally understood her, he said, "Well, please call me as soon as he gets in."

The silence was such a relief he felt a bit better. Perhaps he didn't have to take the day off. Acting on impulses had often worked against him. He went back to the news item.

The news came as no surprise to him. He had known of Bob's "long battle."

As early as 1960 when there was some publicity on Bob's being a three-pack-a-day smoker, following a minor surgery and a subsequent removal of his right lung, Sol wrote him a letter, his first and only letter to Bob, who, possibly, did not read it. Perhaps it was thrown into the wastebasket or passed around as a joke among those in charge of the actor's fan mail. It was written in the passionate language of Sol's favorite American writers (Edgar Allan Poe, Henry Wadsworth Longfellow, William Cullen Bryant, Washington Irving, etc.) whose works he had been taught in Philippine public schools by American teachers. When he first arrived in the States, he could hardly understand the language the people around him spoke. It seemed so different from the way his American teachers spoke in the classroom, his only contact with them; and it didn't sound anything like the language of his favorite writers. What was worse, the first American friends he knew had not heard of his favorite writers. It was frightening. Had he been duped?

In his letter to Robert Taylor, he wrote:

> "First, I should apologize, writing you in this manner, a perfect stranger to you, but maybe I would not be far from wrong if I assume that you are used to receiving letters from strangers to whom you are not a stranger, I mean.

> "This letter is motivated by the noblest of sentiments. Ever since I read of your hospitalization, I have brooded

4

over the workings of fate. Perhaps in the avalanche of fan mail that clutters your doorsteps, this is one of the very few from a man, a manly man like you, who has followed your career closely. Whose own life is somehow linked to yours with a bond that knows no breaking.

"Bob, there are not too many men left in America, in the whole world, I daresay, and it goes without saying that you are such a man, a beautiful manly man. And that is why I want you well and alive. Desist—oh, I beg of you—desist from smoking cigarettes!"

Sol himself did not smoke. But what good did that do him when Bob was surely killing himself. And now he was dead.

Time was of the important, Sol King himself would say, intentionally meaning to be ungrammatical, a verbal way, he hoped, of adjusting to the language of his environment, at first, just joking really, until the statement became a speech habit; and after a while he didn't care, neither did his friends among Filipinos and Americans, but the Americans in particular who found the statement cute and certainly difficult to refute.

He was not saying now, time is of the important, but he was thinking it. As a matter of fact, time was of the *very* important *now.*

Usually in June, during the first days of summer, daily work routine in the stockyard began to slacken a bit so that in the hottest days in July and August, there was a mere scattering of hogs arriving, mostly from northern Iowa, and not in the best of health, suffering from the intense heat, restless and mean until they were fed and watered and bedded down. Around Labor Day, the stockyard was practically closed, with a skeleton force on longer shifts as almost everybody was on vacation. He was among the first to go. "See you in Miami," he would say. He always said that, but he actually never went to Miami or any other place. Most of the time he just stayed home in his apartment on Honore Street, reading travel brochures which described in detail sights and spots and happenings in Miami and other vacation lands. Besides, who went to Miami in summer?

Now he should take a real vacation. No faking this time. See as many of those places in the travel brochures he had hoarded like imitation stones he had been content to own in the absence of the genuine ones. The pictures were so real, it felt like being there. The descriptions of mountains and lakes and valleys

5

sounded like Longfellow's murmuring pines and the hemlocks with the rushing of great rivers through Poe's kingdom by the sea.

In years past he took his vacations as everyone else in the stockyard was supposed to do, particularly in the lean months of July and August. After Labor Day, work started picking up and everybody had stories to tell of fishing in Spirit Lake, boating down the Mississippi, camping in the Black Hills or simply travelling around the country, secure in their old reliable cars with their fantastic mileage per gallon; ecstatic over the gorgeous sights along the way in Boulder, Colorado, or in upper Michigan, unseasonable skiing in Vermont south of the Canadian border. Sol had been to all these places—and more—that is, he had read all the literature about them. He sounded very convincing as he raved over nights under the stars at Lake Tahoe and Yosemite Park, trout fishing in Lake Okoboji, midnight swimming in Higgins Lake in Roscommons, camping in Hiawatha country, although everything he knew about these places came straight from travel folders, advertisements and special travel numbers in magazines and newspaper supplements.

The reason for his staying home and faking all his vacations was his determination to save. He had been a spendthrift in his youth. He had known men like him from the Philippines who ended up paupers in the United States because all they were after was a good time. That was not going to happen to him. No, sir. He had known what it meant to go hungry, without a cent in his pocket and forced to take dangerous and filthy jobs. And nobody need remind him that he was practically alone in the world. He knew. It was the painful truth: he was truly alone. He had no more friends and relatives in the Philippines. It had been such a long time. He had to save. In the first year in the stockyard, he didn't know how long he would be able to keep his job. So he made it a point to record every penny he spent. Every night, before going to bed, he jotted down his expenses for the day, counted his loose change, looked over his budget. As soon as the monthly statement from the bank arrived, he took time going over every item to make sure he did not overlook checks that had not yet been cashed. There had been years in the stockyard when he barely broke even after taxes. But these were better times now. Still he was careful about every cent he spent. He lived well enough, but there were practices that he thought were wasteful. For a time he could not bring himself to throwing away paper cups and paper tissues after each use. Particularly, the paper cups. They were so sturdy, so clean and beautiful, it was criminal to throw them away. And what was insanitary about using the cup again and again, perhaps the whole day? Later, he got used to it. He explained it away to himself, as part of the assimilation process into the American way of life, whatever that meant. He made sure, however, before throwing away each cup, that it was crushed into shapelessness.

Now, in spite of taxes and the rising price of commodities, the pay was so good, he was saving so much more than he had hoped for or imagined. In addition to what was coming to him in social security and retirement annuities, he had money in the bank. Except that today he knew there was not going to be too many more years. Years, did he say? Could he honestly talk in terms of years? Maybe a year or two? Or less. He felt it in the chill that crawled under his skin. There was not much time left.

If the end came, soon or late, whatever, it should find him on the move. Start within the country. Make real all those vacations he had faked. All those lovely sounding names, echoes from the American literature close to his heart, precious to his memory—the Monongahela, the Shadow Mountains, what did they really look like?

No. He didn't think he would be able to work today. Sol folded the newspaper carefully and pressed the button again. This time it was the Boss himself, his voice a squeak above the static.

Honore Street on which he lived was part of an extensive area covering several blocks of a Polish colony where, as far as he knew, he was the only Filipino. How this happened was simple: when he was looking for a place to rent, one of the butchers in the stockyard told him that his son had run away with some girl and Sol could have his room if he wanted it. He didn't stay there long, however. He moved from one apartment to another, but somehow, he never went outside the Polish colony. Sol liked the Polish people, their sweetness, their fatness. They were all like first class hogs, that's how he used to think of them, no insult intended, but it was their sweetness that held him. Like him, they were always talking of home, of the old country, and like him, they were making no move to return.

During his fake vacations he stayed in his apartment and kept himself busy all day arranging and rearranging his file of Manila envelopes, dusting the many plastic things in all the rooms, tinkering with the stereo and taping music from FM programs. He defrosted the refrigerator and cooked himself Philippine foods. Of course, he read travel literature.

Sol put the two pictures side by side on the kitchen table:

8

Robert Taylor, 25, as Armand Duval opposite Greta Garbo's "Camille" in 1937 and as Capt. Mat Holbrooke in "The Detectives," 1967, a long-running TV series. Say thirty years and it seems nothing, now look at these pictures and you don't have to say a word, but you realize what you have not quite acknowledged before.

He shut the door to the living room and stared at his image in the full length mirror on the door: Capt. Holbrook no less, wrinkles and all. What had happened to him? Why had he not known?

Still thinking of time as *of the important*, he was now telling himself, frankly and as unemotionally as he could, that he had come to America alone thirty years ago and now he was still alone. He had liked it that way. Did he, though? The truth was something else.

The apartment, such as it was, could give him the lie. And the other rooms he had lived in, here and there, all over the continent, had he forgotten?

He opened a closet and began searching among the dusty suitcases piled on top of one another above two rows of suits and shirts and coats on hangers suspended from parallel bars. In the dark closet he had difficulty trying to find the string tied to a bulb hanging from the ceiling. He groped and pulled at other things until he found it and in the sudden light, the dust covered his face nearly choking him. He was sure the pictures were somewhere among the clutter, the old ones he had not seen for many years now. A pile of brown envelopes showed through a broken zipper on a frayed dusty two-suiter in brown and green plaid design. As he pulled it away from under two other suitcases, an assortment of packing paper, wire and wooden hangers fell on him, and he said, damn. Finally, however, he found the right suitcase. Most of the envelopes had identifying marks: Receipts, Travel, Important, Pictures (new), Pictures (old). One Manila envelope bore his name in charcoal black ink, others had dates under Miscellaneous.

Sol pulled out the envelope marked Pictures (old) and dusted it with a used shirt sticking out of a laundry bag. Clearing a space on the table where the pictures of Robert Taylor lay, he poured out the contents. A cascade of brown faces rolled out, of boys and girls, alone and in groups, some sharp and clear as though they had been taken and developed only a week earlier, others blurred and unrecognizable, all against backgrounds of bamboo fences and concrete walls pockmarked with holes; smiling faces, mostly strangers now. Who were these, indeed, that once upon a time were deserving of a lay-away plan as business houses put it, mementoes, no doubt, to mark an occasion, but for what?

This one . . . and this . . . soon Sol was occupied in trying hard to identify some of the pictures. In one or two, the recognition, after a while, brought an instant glow, a quick kindling of warmth or nothing, not even a coldness. Then he realized that he was wasting time, allowing himself to be waylaid. He reminded himself of what he was looking for. The faces fell away, surprised, hurt, or just plain comical, as he shoved them aside, looking for one picture, his, taken after a declamation contest. It was formally posed, he recalled; he was dressed in his best white drill suit, and captioned: First Prize Winner, Interscholastic Declamation Contest. He could still recite from memory some of the lines from his winning piece, "The Raven," by Edgar Allan Poe. What he could not recall just now was the face. His fingers went over the pictures again; bending low, he adjusted his glasses. He turned the back of the envelope to be sure it was marked Pictures (old.) It was. Suddenly, from among the faces, one held his attention, a smiling face, dimpled and brown, her black hair in a pony tail, the ribbon on her shoulder the color of dust. He moved his lips as he picked it up. Luz, Luz, he whispered, as he raised the picture to his face as if he were going to kiss it, but instead, he turned the picture over. Her handwriting was small and fine like light bruises. She had written in pencil, hardly legible now. He had to bring it close to the light, but before he could decipher her message, he was reading it aloud from memory: Dear Sol, lest you forget, the Original. Oh, Luz, he cried noiselessly, biting his lips, recalling the last time he had heard about her, American soldiers in her house, her own family selling PX goods in the black market. He put the picture back among the rest on the table, saying damn, damn it, as he started, furiously, to look for his picture again.

As the thought struck him, he realized how stupid he was. Of course, there was another envelope with his name in charcoal black ink. Where else?

There it was, the champion declaimer, straight black hair parted near the middle, above a broad forehead, a happy smile showing a perfect row of white teeth, beneath a high-bridged nose, a gift no doubt from some bastard ancestor who took her new-found religion to bed. Sol's hand trembled a little as he placed the picture beside Robert Taylor's "as a Rising Star in 1936." Look at the twins. Why hadn't anyone remarked on the similarity? All these years. Now it was too late.

He turned around and faced his image again in the mirror on the door. Capt. Holbrooke, at your service. He wished he could laugh. True, there had been illusions enough in his life. But look at him, look at me. That was not all. Some of the women in his life . . . oh, damn, damn it. Sol moved a step towards the mirror. Why had he not known? Why had he missed those lines around the mouth, the chicken folds on his neck, the gray on his head? But it didn't matter too much now. Why should it?

What game was he playing anyhow? He was still sick inside him. He had thrown up everything he had eaten for lunch. In the late evening hour, the sun was still high in the sky, like noon in mid-winter on Honore Street.

The apartment was on the ground level and he had to pass through a narrow opening between the walls of adjoining houses to get to it, unless he came through the rear, a fenced-in yard littered with garbage cans and the parts and chassis of an old car. He didn't mind the narrow lane except when it was raining. An open umbrella was too wide. So now he wore a raincoat. Umbrellas were for sissies, anyhow, it amused him to tell himself. He explained to the girls who complained of the very narrow alley that this way no fat girl would ever make it to his apartment. As he said this, he realized it wasn't true. He had had fat girls visiting him in his apartment. Mostly Polish girls in the neighborhood who must have seen, though they did not say it, his resemblance to Robert Taylor. Or it could be they didn't know the actor.

The door was double-locked, that is, the screen door had a lock like the main door, which opened to the kitchen. When he hurried to work without washing the dishes, the pile of plates and cups and glasses was the first thing he saw on his return in the evening, showing above the sink with the faucet usually leaking. To the right was a two-door refrigerator with a doily on top and right on top of the doily was a plastic flower pot with plastic roses so real, sometimes he wanted to water them. With the exception of the stove, which stood directly in front of the door against the opposite wall, everything in the apartment had a cover of sorts, a frilly, lacy something from the Philippines. These were draped on the arms and seats of chairs, on the throw pillows and on the back of the davenport.

Behind a curtained door was his bedroom which led to the bathroom. Outside the curtains was the living room. A dresser stood against one wall; the other walls, all in beige and bare, were lined with a stereo and a color TV set combination radio-phono in a dark brown cabinet. On the farther side of the room opposite all these gadgets was an upholstered seat beside a floor lamp that looked like a spear in the hand of a disembodied warrior. An imitation leather ottoman lay at the foot of the chair.

On rainy days, he removed his raincoat at the doorstep before entering the kitchen, planting his feet precisely in the center of a throw rug that was supposed to be water absorbent and easy to clean. Folding the raincoat, he was careful the water didn't drip on the floor. He carried it over his head, pushed the curtain in his bedroom, on to the bathroom where he placed it on a hanger over the tub to dry.

The bathroom was carpeted in green from wall to wall. There were Baguio lilies (plastic, as usual) on the cover of the water tank and roses on the window sill. On top of the built-in medicine cabinet was a shawl of indeterminate color and ambiguous origin, perhaps Egyptian or Moorish, most likely, Disneyland. After hanging the raincoat, he would look around and inhale deeply, once or twice, sniffing like a hound, and should he detect a smell that he didn't like, sweat and body odor, cigarette or, worse, the stink of cigar butts, he would begin to spray the polluted rooms with deodorizers, and later emerge from the fog of fragrant mist like a man who had at last found his soul.

Everything in the apartment was in its place, including the back numbers of such magazines as he read, *Time*, *Newsweek*, and his favorite tabloid, the *Enquirer*. These were arranged neatly, each in chronology. Nothing upset him more than to discover an issue missing. Then he spent hours looking for it. Usually it had only been mislaid by a visitor, a guy who had dropped in for a chat or, in times long past, one of his girls who had to go to the bathroom and needed something to read to distract her mind from a stubborn case of constipation.

This was home to him. He found comfort in being here, a kind of warmth in the waiting softness of the davenport, his TV chair, his bed, peace of sorts in the decorated bathroom, in the fragrance of sprayed mist and pine and lavender, the smell of the great outdoors right in his living room, so the advertisements said and they were right. This was home. Where else?

Oh, he knew what home used to mean. Every exile did. Home was always a bit of the faraway land of their birth. No matter how long they stayed in America, they were still Filipinos. The changing seasons and all those promises in expensive cosmetic bottles and tubes had not altered their complexion. Nor his thinking, in Sol's case. Nor his beliefs. His secret knowledge of secret truths. His knowing now, for instance, that it was time to go. Not really making a last fling. He had had all that and more. True, there were times when he hungered for companionship, alternately desiring and abhorring it, fearful of a repetition of what he had run away from many years ago. No more of that. What he had to do now was take charge of time, attempt a calculated spacing of whatever was left of it. At these moments, always he recalled what the poets called the sands of time. If he only knew how much more of it was left. . . . But one thing was definite in his mind: a vacation, a real one, a long one, or as long as those sands lasted. There would be no returning to the stockyards. In his heart, he had said goodbye to all his friends there. Anyway, the stockyards were going, too. The signs had been there long ago. He knew. The men that ran the stockyards were not saying anything yet, but they knew. The end was in sight. Soon the huge mazes of pens would be empty. The cars and vans that brought the animals were seldom full to capacity and they were no longer coming regularly. It was all right for him to go. He was just leaving a little earlier. The sign was there and he had recognized it for what it was. Goodbye then. No hard feelings. Now what to do? Where to go?

Discover America. No, Sol, not that. That's a gimmick phrase. No gimmicks this time. Discover, period. Find out. The last moments should be an activation of what had lain fallow for so long, a clearing of the air in the human spirit of what pollutes it and destroys it in the end, a discovery, indeed. What was that again, he asked himself, listening to his thoughts. A hell of a way of saying that now what mattered most was to live well every moment of what yet remained.

Sol walked to the pictures on the table. It was past eight in the evening, but it was still like day outside on Honore Street.

❧

$\mathscr{L}$

Wherever people gathered and introductions went the rounds, Sol invariably introduced himself as "Solomon King, butcher," saying it without any hint of shame or embarrassment, nor of pride. Among his countrymen, he identified himself thus, saying it as though reading from a calling card. He had seen many Filipinos exchanging calling cards. If he had found a need for such cards, that was what he was going to have printed, "Solomon King, Butcher." What else was there to print? There were those who thought he was joking as though he had said, "Solomon King, Crook." You're joking, they insisted. No, that's a fact, Sol said.

This, however, was not the absolute truth. He had started as a menial and later became a butcher. At the time he had decided to take a terminal vacation, he was a supervisor of operations. In his mezzanine office, suspended like a rectangular glass cage on cables over the length and breadth of the slaughterhouse, he could say that he had worked himself up, literally.

In his first year in the stockyards, he had to clean the pens in the compound. He sprayed hot water from a hose into the pens after the animals had been removed for slaughter to get

14

the pens ready for the next batch. He wore gloves and sweated a lot even in winter.

When he saw how the hogs were butchered, he felt no qualms about the blood, the killing. It was almost scientific unlike the way they butchered animals in the Philippines. Soon he was part of the butchering crew and from then on, moved from one function to another in the same area until he was promoted to supervisor which entitled him, among other things, to that cage above all that carnage.

But he had been at many other jobs as he moved from city to city until finally settling down in Chicago. He loved the city. It was here that he first landed, arriving by bus from a coastal town in the south. He had his first jobs here. Then he moved on to wherever he felt like staying for as long or as short as circumstances allowed. New York, California, Washington D.C. Other states, the big and the small cities. He stayed in some of these places hoping it would be for good. But somehow, he just had to keep going. He thought he was going to stay put in Washington D.C., but one day, he found himself returning to Chicago. Before long, somehow he knew that this time, it was going to be Chicago to the end. Even now, should he finally get going on a return trip of sorts to places he had known, Chicago was to remain his base unless time ran out before he could make it back.

It was downtown Chicago that called to him most of the time, the business district where there was movement and a spell and as far as he was concerned, without boundaries and directions. Until now he could not tell for certain what the northside or southside was except that they were opposites as were the east and the west and that State and Madison cut the city in two.

Of course, he knew where he lived, in the southside, but he was not sure where it was or what it was. Maps frightened him, particularly the map of Chicago, which looked, to him, like a diseased epidermis with exposed veins and arteries in decay where the blood had long clotted in areas that were supposed to be parks and landmarks of a famous city.

On the first day of his long vacation, instead of going directly to the company doctor with whom he had a morning appointment, he left the apartment early and took a bus for the downtown district. This was not the first time he had done this. He felt good, himself a moving point among a swirl of other points in the pulse of a city, breathlessly alive. The sights went through him like a miracle drug: the changing lights in any hour of the day advertising names and products, giving the time and the temperature. The tall men, the long-limbed women, the ever young and golden goddesses. He used to be thankful he had lived at a time when skirts were high and breasts were free to bob up and down like round fruits at Maytime, their lovely weight firm in his grasp. Not any more. When navels stared at him, he stared back in tearful frustration. Then there were the desperate and ancient men and women, wandering like him, looking for a sign perhaps, some kind of strength for a wasted body, a flash of recognition from a blankly staring sky. He had strange sensations: the buildings, towers, temples, and churches were crumbling at his touch; bridges and highways were falling apart, mere threads and cardboard pieces easily unstuck. But actually, there was no strength in him, a weakness, yes, in what was once a massive energy from a body that had not been aware of time passing.

He stayed on the sidewalks close to the buildings. In winters, he needed the warmth; on this sunny June morning, he wanted the shade. The show windows held gifts that seemed within his reach. After a while, the exertion wearied him and a dreary sameness covered everything. He sought out those sites where buildings were being wrecked or built. When there was nothing as yet showing above plywood and board enclosures and all the action was underground, Sol looked for openings between the boards and planks through which he could watch workmen grimy with mud, driving piles of logs and concrete into the ground. It seemed an endless task, but after a while, beams and cranes rose above the enclosures, steel arms spread-eagled against the sky like monstrous scarecrows.

He had once worked as an unskilled laborer on a high-rise building under construction near the old post office. Just arrived in Chicago, he was running low on funds and desperately in need of a job.

The first time he was up on a beam connecting base plates for a welder companion whom he was supposed to assist, a taciturn redhead who chewed tobacco and spit down the street, he was scared in spite of the security belt around his waist and the Red Wings shoes he had borrowed for the day. It was like standing on a mountain top in a new country. He wondered whether it was not better to die of hunger than to perish that way. He was sure he was not going to live through the afternoon. The next day there was a wind blowing and thick clouds got between the beam he was standing on and the street below. The welder had been swallowed up in the low floating clouds. Sol wanted to scream, he wanted to cry, he wished he were back in the Philippines selling lithographs or candies, anything, anywhere, but not up there where but for lack of wings, he felt like a disoriented angel. To this day he didn't know how he had lasted two days on the job.

He knew it was already too late to keep his appointment. He would make excuses. The brilliant doctor would understand, he knew what a coward Sol was, keeping his pains to himself as if by so doing, he would be cured of whatever ailed his body. He just wanted to take a walk.

Sol listened to the tearing and the building going on. The sound came to him from every direction, gradually merging with the increasing roar of traffic. He watched without envy the men on girders looking like puppets. As the rush of traffic subsided later that morning, he heard quite clearly the throb of rivets boring into steel, and it seemed the ground on which he stood shook a little. He had known the giddiness up there, a tiny shaking of the ground below was nothing.

Good doctor, he mused, I'm paying a last call in these remaining days of my life to this city that had been home in the sweetest and cruellest way, after a long affair that could not be helped for whatever it was. Please, understand.

On the site on West Sheridan Road where a twenty-five-story apartment complex now stood, there used to be a funeral home. Sol worked here, too, after the few dollars he received for two days riding steel beams up in the air over the city, had been spent. His eyes had begun to hurt poring over the want-ads sections of Chicago papers. There was nothing he found suitable for him. Then he saw something he didn't quite understand.

The ad said simply: "Wanted, assistant mortician, no experience necessary." He had no idea what a mortician was supposed to do and he didn't care. What seemed promising was that no experience was necessary.

On his way to West Sheridan Road, all he prayed for was that he get the job and, hopefully, it was done, whatever it was, on the ground. He wouldn't mind in his desperate need if it involved a little digging. As it turned out, it was, indeed, somehow related, in a sort of inevitable way, to digging.

Sol stood under the sign: Swingle's Funeral Home. Is this it, he asked himself, peering close at the small type of the clipping he held. Opposite the home, across the street, was a motorcycle dealer. He hoped there had been a mistake, that, in fact, it was the motorcycle dealer who needed a mortician. As he stood between the two buildings, baffled and undecided, a dark man, with tousled graying hair and a peaked nose, appeared at the doorway of the funeral home.

"Yes?" the man asked. His eyes bulged as if there were too much of them.

"Yes," Sol answered, adding quickly, "sir. Yes, sir." He extended his hand to show the man the clipping, but withdrew it immediately. The man didn't seem interested. He was staring at Sol's face.

"You . . . sir," Sol began and paused as he glanced significantly at the sign over the door.

"Yes, yes," the man said, which only deepened Sol's confusion.

"Yes," Sol said. It was catching. But he was not making any progress. It was late afternoon and he had had nothing to eat all day. A bold statement was necessary. "I'm your assistant mortician," he said, adding rather indecisively, "No experience necessary."

"Yes. Yes," the man repeated, but this time he uttered the word in a different key. His lips were partly open as in a smile, a no-good smile. He was making fun of him. Of course. Naturally. Sol had made a fool of himself, making such a silly introduction. At this point, he was beginning to have a general idea of the nature of the job.

"I mean, sir," Sol explained, "I'm answering your ad for an assistant mortician."

"Yes, yes," the man said, then bowing with a flourish, added, "Enter," his hand leading Sol into a small room that looked like a church with pews and candlesticks. It smelled of withered flowers. Sol glanced back towards the motorcycle shop on the other side of the street longingly, as the door closed behind him.

Somehow he still held hopes that an assistant mortician arranged the flowers or breathed life into them, cut the wick off the huge candles. These were real candles, not bulb-tipped electric bars.

It was not until the man had led him to a back door which opened to the basement that Sol's apprehension turned into panic. The man had crooked a finger and Sol wanted to cry out, no, no, but he was too stunned to protest. Down in the basement, he realized the immensity of his mistake. Perhaps it were better up there among the clouds than down here among the dead.

There were cadavers all over the place, on long tables, in open coffins. Everywhere. There must have been another massacre in Chicago. Wherever he looked, there was a dead body, both male and female in mixed company. The one nearest the foot of the stairway was naked, an old man with a white beard and a crooked nose. Sol turned towards the man who had led him down to this land of the dead, afraid that he had disappeared and become the dead man, so much did they look alike; except for the beard, he could have been only playing alive. But there he was. Quickly, Sol's eyes turned to the naked wasted body, the pubic hair, lush and curly, the man's genitals, a dead worm in the jungle growth.

The man beside him said something that sounded like a question, but Sol did not quite get it.

"Beg pardon?" Sol said, adding senselessly like a robot, "No experience necessary." Why, he had become a robot. He was saying things he didn't mean to say. Maybe he was already dead himself, a cadaver on its feet.

"What is your name?" the man was asking.

"My name," he began, like a school boy back in the Philippines, "is Solomon King."

"Solomon?"

"Sol for short."

"I know." He bent down to look close at his face, perhaps to listen to the growling in his stomach. "You're not Jewish?"

"What's Jewish?" Sol replied quickly.

"No. I thought not. You can't be."

The more he looked at the man, the more certain he felt that the cadaver with the beard was a close relative, maybe a brother.

"I'm Mr. Swingle, the mortician," the man was saying. There was no grief on his face, only a weariness in the bloodshot eyes and the feeble voice.

"My prayer's answered," Mr. Swingle continued. "I've been working since last night. I can't any more. I'm finished. And you're here, the answer."

"How do you do, Mr. Swingle," Sol said to formalize the introduction.

"You're hired," Mr. Swingle said. "Me, I'm finished. For today, I'm pooped. Now, I've begun to work on this one . . ." He pointed to his naked relative. Sol noticed a pump attached

20

with a rubber tubing to the man's body.

He wanted to run away. He felt dizzy and he wanted to vomit. Holding his stomach that churned emptily, he thought he was going to cry. God, this is no way, he was thinking.

"You'll get used to it," Mr. Swingle said, watching Sol holding his stomach and staring at the end of the rubber tubing inside a hole in the cadaver.

Sol turned away, shaking his head.

"Take it easy. No problem. Once you get used to it. What are all these bodies anyhow? Objects. Things. Nothings. Come, I'll show you," the mortician said in a low confident voice.

Sol said nothing, but he was listening. And thinking. So many bodies. Where did they come from? He would have heard of the massacre if there had been one. Was there an epidemic he had not heard about? Up to then, he had not seen anybody dying or dead in America. Once, on a street in San Francisco, he saw a long funeral procession. He didn't know what it was. It was noon time and all the cars had their lights on and he had inquired. When told what it really was, he said, more to himself than the man he had addressed, "So. Even Americans die." In the street where he lived in the Philippines, there was a daily procession of the dead borne in a coffin on the shoulders of pall bearers, followed by a motley crowd on foot. The bereaved family were all dressed in black. You could hear their wailing kilometers away. Well, that was not done in the States. People didn't show their grief. Perhaps it was bad manners. It could be they did not grieve enough to cry.

"This pump here pumps out the blood. Now watch."

The man had stooped over the body and began to pump the blood out. Sol watched the red blackish fluid trickle into a pail. Then the man stopped and pulled Sol towards the body, saying, "Now, you pump."

He did as he was told, but he didn't have the energy. He wanted to tell him, "I can't. I'm too weak. I haven't eaten anything," but he knew he could not eat now, not with all this. Sol kept pumping.

"Harder, harder," the man said, and Sol, in spite of himself and everything, obliged.

"You'll do," Mr. Swingle said. "Now, when you're through, we'll do this."

He opened a set of drawers and took out several knives and ·before Sol knew what the man was doing, Mr. Swingle had ripped open the dead man's middle. It was a bloody mess. With long rubber gloves, he drew out all the internal organs and dropped them in another bucket.

"Just watch," he kept saying.

Sol must have passed out because when he became aware of the operation, the mortician had already sutured the wound. "Now, press some of that cotton here," he was saying.

Sol did not move. His hands lay limp on his sides and his head had fallen on his breast.

"What's the matter, are you sick?" the man asked. "Come on now. Nothing to it. First time is always hard. But you'll get over it. Now, watch, watch this."

Without any effort of will or body, Sol's eyes followed every movement the man made, his words coming to him as through the screen of a confessional. Perhaps he was being told the holiest things, repent, be contrite, repent. What he heard was something else, though.

"Then we pump this solution into the body, make sure the stitches are taut. Now choke the wound with more cotton. So. More cotton in the ears, the mouth, every opening, so the solution don't seep out. There. Nothing to it."

From another drawer, the mortician drew out a complete make-up kit and began to put rouge on the cheeks, closing the dead man's eyes gently, touching the eyelids a bit, the eyebrows, too. Like an artist, he drew back a step to admire his work, smiling with satisfaction. "How do you like that? He has never looked better in life. When his relatives and friends come, they'll say, look, like he's only fast asleep."

By now Sol had recovered enough to be able to help put on the suit, an elegant blue gray complete with vest and boutonniere. The dead man appeared stiffly dignified and clean with none of the pallor of death. The mortician's art had breathed life into the emptied carcass. Any moment now the body would arise, the man's lips utter words like "Give me my cane," and walk away towards the lakeshore.

"This is Judge Samuel Krotz, retired," Mr. Swingle said. He must have realized he had not been proper for failing to introduce the cadaver to his assistant after all the intimacy. "And we retire him." With these words, he pushed the metal shelf on which the body had been dressed and made up, towards a vault, which closed with a screech. "We'll keep him there until we're ready to put him in his coffin."

The relatives and friends were due some time that evening

and there were five others that Mr. Swingle had not worked on. But with Sol around, he seemed relieved.

"What country you come from, hey?"

"The question startled Sol at first, but he had been asked the same repeatedly. His answer was quick, almost automatic. "Philippine Islands. Philippines. I'm a Filipino."

"What's that? Christian?"

"Sometimes, sir."

"Ah! Good enough. I like you. You stay? My assistant, he disappear just like that." Mr. Swingle swung his arm in a parabola of disdain. Sol thought the gesture was very picturesque, but he wished the man would stop baby-talking to him.

"I taught him. The works. Good student, too. But just when I thought he was beginning to enjoy his work—why, sometimes I heard him singing while he worked—then he quit. No notice. Nothing. Oh, well, I guess, in a job like this, when you begin to sing at work, it's time to quit."

That's it, that's the way to talk, Sol was saying to himself as he listened when all of a sudden, the man concluded rather abruptly, "Me, I dong sink," or something that sounded as funny.

Sol had decided by then that he would not show up the next day. Just how Mr. Swingle seemed able to read his thoughts was a mystery. It could have been coincidence or a combination of that and the man's instinctive understanding of human nature, but what happened was that Sol didn't have a chance.

They had supper together. On the loft or balcony, a mezzanine-like upper room, was a daybed, kitchen, and bath above the ground floor where the coffins lay at right angles to one another, each surrounded by pews and candelabra.

"We have supper together, you like?" was how Mr. Swingle had phrased his invitation.

Although he had already made up his mind about quitting, Sol felt he was entitled to a meal, at least, for what he had been through. He was no longer hungry, however, and he didn't think he could eat, but he wanted to, he had to.

It was a light supper, but it felt good. The hot soup had a lot of onions in it, which he liked. The salami sandwich was filling.

Mr. Swingle talked all through the meal about the mortician's art, its contribution in easing the pain that death brings to those left behind, the good it does to the human body, like there had been no death at all. His art made it possible for death to look like just another stage in a man's life, a transition, with the body seemingly intact, like the dead had dropped in at the funeral home for a fitting, a beauty treatment, a cure. The mortician learns to view life and death without the burdens and hazards that sentiment brings.

"I see the body, is all, the blood pumped out, the solution pumped in, what for you ask. Surely not to give life, the solution can't do that, but it preserves the look of life for as long as desired. I charge accordingly. More expensive with all the trimmings. Business. Like wedding, you give more money to ring the bells, no? Yes. I'm doctor, priest, rabbi, magician, too, small god. I make the dead look warm, alive, like the heart's beating all right."

The man barely touched his food. It was obvious the supper was for Sol, to make him like the job, so that he would stay.

"I teach you the art for free. Better, you earn as you learn. You live here. You eat with me. Free. Golly, you're young. I'm old. The bereaved family looks at me and thinks of death. The young mortician does better."

Sol liked the idea of free room and board. That should help while he looked around for another job. He would have stayed had Mr. Swingle not been too kind to him. One night after supper, he told Sol, "You're a beautiful man."

"Thank you, sir."

"Seriously. Perhaps you got lots of girls, right?"

"Oh, well . . ."

"You could be an actor. As a matter of fact, you remind me of one."

But Mr. Swingle could not remember whom he looked like. The phone rang and on his way to answer it, he held Sol's shoulders with a passionate grip that sickened him. After getting his week's wages, he quit.

A Philippine wake is an occasion for merriment. The room where the dead lies in repose is brightly lighted, usually with extra electric bulbs on extension cords attached to a neighbor's house. Food and drink are served to everybody who calls, Chinese crackers, noodles for long life, strong hot coffee to keep awake. A vigil is kept all night till morning or for as long as the wake lasts, which takes days when the dead is embalmed. Tables are set up around the coffin and foursomes play cards or mahjong for money. There is an endless flow of entertainment, which includes a game called Riddle, Riddle, What Am I?

Question: A pretty lady surrounded with swords.
Answer: Pineapple.
Question: We clap and clap but are not heard.
Answer: Eyelids.

A small space at the head of the coffin is allowed the chief mourner to listen to her grief if she could.

Robert Taylor was buried Wednesday of the same week. Governor Ronald Reagan of California delivered the eulogy. After that, there was nothing more said in the papers about him, not in any of the Chicago papers that Sol read.

In the doctor's clinic where he was waiting for his turn, there were magazines, many months old. The company doctor had referred him to Dr. Noah Harm. Sol had arrived a few minutes before the 11 o'clock appointment. Now it was fifteen minutes after and all he had seen were nurses who looked very healthy. The phones were always ringing. The waiting room was nearly full of old people like him. For the first time he was aware that he looked like any other old person. He fitted in well with the crowd. Some were on crutches. Those that didn't have any walked like aged toddlers. Some had bandaged arms or legs in casts. He looked well among them. They were all white except for a brown man in a corner, reading *Life* magazine. He could be Indian or Mexican. Perhaps Filipino. He wore a winter suit, which was all right because the room was air-conditioned, but out there in the blazing streets . . . But perhaps he had an air-conditioned car. Or it could be that his sickness required keeping warm at all times. The brown man closed the magazine and turned towards Sol. His face was heavily wrinkled, the texture of leather, an embalmed body without the beauty treatment. As their eyes met, Sol smiled. When he felt pain all over his body, anything he did hurt, except smiling. There was no effort, it was easy, in his case, involuntary, and nice, especially if his smile was returned, like now. Smiling, the man limped toward him and extended his hand.

"You're Filipino," the man said with some authority, appointing him as such even if he were something else. "I'm Colonel Jess Padiya." His grip was strong and a smell like cigar butts went with his handshake. An indistinguishable button stuck out like embossed print from the lapel of his winter jacket.

Sol stood up as he mumbled his name and felt quite a relief when the colonel let go of his hand. He handed Sol a card. They both sat down while Sol read what was printed on it. Four different seals appeared above the name:

Col. Jesus Padilla, AFP, Ret.
Veteran of World Wars I & II
LIFE MEMBER

Residence:

| Balut, Tondo, Mla. | Friendship, Wis. |
| PHILIPPINES | U.S.A. |

Each seal had its own emblem with the words: Philippine Veterans Legion, American Legion, Reserve Officers Legion of the Philippines, and AFP Retired Veterans Association, Incorporated.

"You don't live in Chicago," Sol said, pocketing the card.

"No. Just visiting. What did you say your name is?"

"Solomon King. I'm a retired butcher. Or soon will be."

"You're joking. I mean, you don't look old enough to retire."

"Oh, I'm old enough."

"Guess how old I am?"

Sol hesitated. The man looked like he was one hundred years old. But he couldn't say that. Besides, the man was strong in spite of his limp. He could still feel the pressure of the man's handshake.

"I'm eighty-two," the colonel said with a chuckle. "On the

21st of August, a little over two months from now, I shall be eighty-three. So you could say I'm eighty-three." He took one of the cigars sticking out of his breast pocket and offered it to Sol.

"No, thanks," Sol said politely.

"Princess Margaret and I have the same birthday," he said, laughing aloud over some private joke, no doubt, as he put back the cigar in his pocket.

Sol glanced at his watch. It was almost 11:30. "I've never been here before. Have you?"

"Oh, yes," the colonel said.

"What time is your appointment?"

"Me? I have no appointment. I just come in here to rest my leg."

Sol heard his name called. He excused himself and followed the nurse inside a swinging door. She led him to one of the rooms and told him to wait. "Meanwhile, you may remove your clothes and wait for Dr. Harm. He'll be in shortly."

"Everything?" Sol asked.

The nurse consulted the papers in her hand. "I guess so," she said after a while, closing the door after her.

He sat on a stool near a table attached to a corner on which was a lamp and a desk calendar. The room was private enough and quiet except for a purring sound as from an exhaust or an air-conditioner. The door had shut noiselessly. There was no sound of any door banging shut anywhere in the building. A medicine cabinet stood beside what looked like an operating table covered with a clean white sheet. A stethoscope and an instrument for measuring blood pressure called by a name he had never been able to pronounce, dangled above the table. Everything was spotlessly clean and the air smelled like lysol with a trace of lemon. As he tried to reach for a hanger, he bumped against a porcelain chamber so sparklingly clean one could have eaten out of it. Neatly folded towels hung over a silver rod. He undressed slowly, looking in the mirror over a sink.

He was thin, flabby. God, he was old. Suddenly old. In spite of his body pains, he didn't have to see this doctor. All he wanted to consult was the company doctor because he was applying for a long, extended leave of absence. After looking him over cursorily, Doc told him to see Dr. Harm, a gerontologist, he would take care of him. Sol trusted doctors, but there was something they didn't know, in his case, his secret truth, which only he knew, no one else. God maybe. Yes. God. He had prayed since that Sunday. Could he be wrong? It was God who could say, but God didn't say. It must be the truth. It was the truth. He knew as no one else did that his life and Bob's were one, in a manner of saying, one's life was an extension of the other. It must sound crazy, but it was not. There had been incontrovertible instances to prove it in his life. Dr. Harm didn't know a thing. Poor Dr. Harm.

The doctor was a young man, short, chubby, and beardless, like a teen-age eunuch, but his voice was deep, resonant as if his tone control was always on sharp. He had introduced himself with a wettish handshake, so unlike the colonel's, it had startled him. "I'm sorry to have kept you waiting," he said. "How are you today? I see you have stripped. Tell me if this is too cold for you."

"No, it's all right," Sol said, pushing down his jockey shorts.

"You don't have to," the doctor said, stopping him. "I have your papers here. I just want to make sure the records are up to date."

He read off some of the items in Sol's record, loud enough for him to hear. "Solomon King, age 62 . . ." he gave Sol a playful look, saying, "You don't look your age, sir. The moment I saw you, I thought perhaps you didn't belong in gerontology . . . let's see . . ." and he turned to the papers once more . . . "Filipino. Height 5'9", weight 160. When was the last time you weighed yourself?"

Sol could not remember. He didn't know he weighed 160 pounds.

"Let's see," Dr. Harm said, pulling a weighing scale from under the sink. The doctor watched the scale as Sol stepped on it. "No, don't bend, stand straight. That's it. 143. You've lost some, but that's good."

Sol got off the scale and returned to the stool.

"No. Sit over there," the doctor said, pointing to the long table. He had unhooked the stethoscope.

"Shall I lie down?"

"No. Not yet."

Then he proceeded to listen to his body sounds or whatever doctors listened to with that instrument. Sol thought the doctor smelled of talcum powder.

"How do you feel? Where are the pains?"

"The pains, doctor? All over my body. They travel. On the arms, the joints. Feel my knees. On the chest, at the back, the neck. It's not just pain, but worse, painspainspainspains. I wonder how I survive. This week I had dizzy spells. . . . "

"You undergo regular examination, physical and medical, at the stockyards, but maybe I should give you another thorough examination, your blood, your stool, your heart, e.e.n.t., okay? Could you come back tomorrow? Now let's see your blood pressure."

"It's a bit elevated." This, after a grim silence.

"I've been tense, doctor."

"Take it easy. There's nothing to worry about. So. I'll see you tomorrow. What time would be convenient for you? Any time? Would 10 o'clock be all right with you?

"Yes, doctor."

"Fine. Put on your clothes now. On your way out tell the nurse at the desk that you have an appointment with me tomorrow at ten. Goodbye."

The colonel's card fell on the floor as he was putting on his shirt. As he bent down to get it, he thought he would pass out. He had to hold on to the sink and he had difficulty getting up. Perhaps he should tell the doctor. But the doctor knew. He had told him about his dizzy spells. There was no help. As the doctor said, take it easy. Keep calm.

He walked carefully on the carpeted floor. The nurse at the desk gave him a card on which she had written his name and the doctor's and the time for the next appointment. He put the reminder in his pocketbook. And remembering the colonel's card, which he had placed in one of his pockets, he also placed it there.

There were still a few patients in the waiting room, but the colonel was no longer there.

A strong wind was whipping up from the lakeshore as he stepped out. Perhaps he should have worn a jacket, too, he mused, like the colonel.

✲

In many villages far from Manila, children play a game of oranges among themselves. They would ask a likely victim, "Do you want to see Manila?" When the child answers, "Yes," someone, usually an earlier victim himself, presses the rind of an orange and squirts the juice into the child's eyes.

As the child screams in pain, rubbing his eyes, the children jump around him like little animals.

The child stops crying soon enough and looks for his first victim.

For Sol filling up forms was a major task. The forms that he had to fill since his arrival in the United States overwhelmed him so much that he began to dread the very idea of having to accomplish one. The instructions that had to be read before following specific instructions were all in print so small he had to strain his eyes reading them. Pages after pages. A blank space is no answer to a question. Write "not required" instead. All that bunk. But he had to fill them because they were required before a lot of things he needed could be given to him, if at all. And there were penalties for failure to do so. Requirements. Penalties. These were dreadful words to him. To the natives, too, he learned in due time.

After all these years he should have no difficulty now. True. But the distaste was still there. He spent hours on various forms in connection with the long—the word was "terminal" on page one—vacation he was taking. There were additional forms for the new doctor to whom he had been referred, not to mention bank forms, information sheets, insurance forms, accident, sickness, hospitalization, etc. The blank on beneficiaries or whom to notify in case of accident or death was always a problem.

He had difficulty recalling the names of relatives, cousins numberless times removed, a favorite uncle—just why favorite he now had no idea and he could care less—friends, acquaintances, who, most probably, didn't even remember him. In his younger days when the thought of death rarely entered his mind, he put down any name, invented relationships and addresses or copied actual names that sounded Filipino and their addresses from the telephone directory. In imagination, he saw the beneficiaries express surprise, at first, over the windfall, trying to recall just who he was and why he had been so kind to make them his beneficiary; and later admitting against the prodding of their conscience, that, indeed, they knew a Solomon King. Did he not sing those naughty songs? Was he not the wise one? The wise one, indeed!

Sol had fun with his "ghost" beneficiaries as he often referred to them in his mind. The game, for to him it was no less, no more than that, never failed to amuse him and somehow reduced some of the distaste he felt for the so-called required forms. Eventually, however, he left the space on beneficiary blank as he was certain that in the end there would be nothing, not much anyway, he would be leaving behind. His mind had been made up. He would give away as much as he could for as long as there was time. There might be time for most of the things he wanted to do. Hopefully. Sometimes he felt he would be given to know when the end was at hand. There was always some one from among the beloved dead who would come to him in a dream and bid him welcome, who would offer him the final gift for the homeward journey. Crazy idea? Perhaps. Oh, but he knew.

To the question whom to notify in case of accident or death, he had only one answer now: First National Bank, Chicago, Illinois.

Filling up forms always served to remind him how little he knew of his parents. He didn't know who his grandparents were on either the maternal or the paternal side. Nor did he know his own parents' birthdays. Of course, they were poor peasants, forced to live in the city of Manila. They had no time nor the money to celebrate anniversaries, including the luxury—that was what it amounted to—of remembering dates. That he knew his own birthday was a fortuitous result of having to give it every time he registered for enrollment in school. But he never had anyone, until he came to America, greet him on his birthday. The first one ever to send him a card in the States on the occasion of his birthday was an insurance company. The greeting served to remind him how old he was and how much he owed the company when his premium payment fell due. That policy had since lapsed because, after a while, he realized there was no need for it.

The simpler forms called for nothing more than the full names. It was easy. In his fine hand he printed opposite Father: Daniel King. Mother: Miguela Sese. Their address was altogether a peculiar matter. He had to write *dead* and later *diseased*. Now he knew the difference. One was diseased usually before one became deceased. One of his classmates in high school in the Philippines gave the declension of the adjective *sick* as sick, sicker, dead. Their old American teacher went into hysterics. He could see her now, bending double and very red of face. There were moments and gestures in the past that had never faded in his memory. Yet every time he tried to recall his father's face, he drew a blank. A scent, yes. Cheap wine, cigarette butts, sweat dried on the skin in the sun. A gesture, a grimace: open palms lashing at him as Sol raised his hands, face averted against the blows. And the voice: never above a whisper. A thin breath of curses as his blows found their mark or a whip crawled alive on Sol's flesh, tracing welts.

Although a mere carpenter and street sweeper on a daily wage, the name Daniel King was well known in Sulucan. He was an expert fencer, a champion in *arnis* as the native fencing practiced in those parts was known. Sol had never seen anything like it. There were not too many who knew what it was like except a few in Sulucan where it must have originated and flourished. Unfortunately, it went away when the violent times came, a victim of the wars, of a continually improving effectiveness of modern weaponry.

Arnis was like a mime. The fencers were classified on a ladder system, with Daniel King occupying the highest rung of the ladder. Those who attained the next step were eligible to challenge him. His frequent opponent was a tall stout man who wheezed when he breathed. His teeth were stained black with betel nut. The man's eyes gave Sol nightmares. He feared and hated them. They shone with malevolence. They would never know tears nor close in death. Now and then, without so much as a sign, the man would pause in the middle of the combat and sip white wine, placed on a nearby stool near the arena, which, usually, was a backyard or a vacant lot outside the walls of the Manila Railroad Company in Sulucan.

Each of the two fighters was armed with two pieces of wood,

neatly rounded, one, dagger short, and the other, long like a spear.

There was a panel of judges—ancient, wizened men—who had held championship titles in their days. They wore cheap graded glasses framed in ordinary wire and attended to their judicial duties with all the concentration the match apparently required if they were to be fair in proclaiming the winner at every encounter.

The audience was mostly pedestrian, but *afficionados* could be distinguished by the manner they expressed approval, surprise or criticism vocally at every turn the contest took. Vocal reaction of this sort was contrary to an established rule of the tournament and so they had to be reminded occasionally by some of the judges. Aside from being distracted by such loud commentary, the judges could be accused of being influenced in their judgment by the afficionados. But sometimes the reaction was so spontaneous, a roar of approval, a stamping of the feet, the beating on wood or tin cans, the clapping of hands, that the judges usually ignored the breach.

Daniel King and his opponent took their wooden arms and walked to any corner of the field just so they stood diagonally to each other. The referee stood in the middle of the court, raised his hands to signify "ready" and dropped them to his sides with an exaggerated cutting of the air. And the fight was on.

The fencers flourished their arms in various angles, curves, parabolas and whatever geometric position was possible or necessary, while they bent forward, backward or sideways depending upon the movement of whoever happened to be on the offense or on the defense at the time. They bent a knee as if genuflecting to kiss a bishop's ring, tilted their bodies sideways in a visual parody of a popular folk-dance, or raised themselves gradually until they had stretched to their full height and were now, it would seem, gazing over a neighbor's fence into a yard where their runaway rooster had strayed. All these, meanwhile flourishing their arms in a set pattern or rhythm the two bodies fell into after a few minutes. Yet they never touched each other as they were not allowed by the rules to move closer than within a yard. To the uninitiated, like Sol, the movements were ludicrous and meaningless. The finale came soon after the two fencers went into a frenzy of gestures with their arms followed by a sudden complete cessation of bodily movements as though each had turned into a stone. This lasted a few seconds as each held his breath while the sweat of their bodies turned the ground at their feet into a puddle. Then at the first hint of life from each, the crowd roared, the judges went into a quick huddle, and without loss of time the referee proclaimed Daniel King was winner and still champion. The vanquished embraced the victor and they toasted each other. Soon the others joined while the children, like Sol, moved away, wondering as always, what it was all about.

It was sad, Sol realized now more than ever, that his father, who was not good in anything else like supporting his wife and only son, was official champion of a silent duel of no touch.

Sol was still in the grades when his father died in a distant province in Mindanao where he had gone presumably to work on an American-owned pineapple plantation. Sol was not sure whether the body was ever brought home. He had never seen his father dead.

Soon after, his mother died, too. He remembered her better. He could see her face now. Unfortunately he had no picture of either of them, alone or in a group. But his mother's face had remained in his memory, a permanent plate, guaranteed not to fade for life, smiling eyes, too round for an Oriental, and too bold; her complexion, too light for a native, but then, she was descended, so he heard, from a long line of mixed races, with the Spanish leaving its indelible mark in the proud nose and the passionate blood. She embraced her religion as did her ancestors their Castilian lovers. A religious fanatic, she died in church, on her knees, her head between her hands on the communion rail after thirty days of continuous fasting.

It didn't seem he had any parents at all. Except in moments like these days when he wrote their names to complete required forms, he seldom thought of them. Thinking of them now, he realized he was older than they were at the time of their passing. Somehow it struck him as odd, funny.

— *Philippine Consulate. . .*

— *Hello. We got problem.*

— *Beg pardon? Who's calling please?*

— *I'm a Filipino. Like my friend here.*

— *Whom did you want to talk to?*

— *We have a argument, see? About Philippine independence . . .*

— *Hold on, please. I'll give you the Cultural Attache . . .*

— *Quiet! She's giving us something.*

— *Office of the Cultural Attache. . .*

— *Hello. Like I say, we got problem. My friend here says Philippine independence is July fourth. I says it's June 19, Rizal's birthday. We got a bet, see?*

— *Sorry. You lose, both of you. It's June 12.*

— *We lose, both of us. Draw. Hey, how come June 12?*

— *It's a long story.*

$\mathcal{V}$

$\mathbb{A}$lthough he had an invitation to attend a "Grand Reception and Ball" at the La Salle Hotel, celebrating the anniversary of the independence of the Republic of the Philippines, Sol decided not to attend after giving it much thought. He had nothing to do that day, but he was not feeling well. Every morning, he woke up stiff and unable to move without pain. Sometimes he felt nauseated. The pains kept him awake nights. He had to take pills more often than he knew for a fact was good for him. There were bottles and tubes of ointment, aspirin of various trademarks, darvon, tylenol, all temporary pain killers, on his bedroom dresser, on the commode near his bed, on the ledge on the wall side of the bathtub, on top of the water tank in the bathroom. They were all over the apartment. Sometimes he mistook those in tubes for toothpaste or hair cream. The brief respite from pain they allowed him was welcome. He was beginning to require stronger doses to be effective.

It was, as he had described his ailment to his doctor, not just pain, but painspainspainspains. Yet he could have attended the reception and ball if he wished. But he was sure it would be no different from last year's celebration, which he had attended.

The same old timers like him would be there as in previous gatherings. There was something in these affairs that made them look like exclusively for the old. There were more young Filipinos now in America, but they had what they called their own happenings. For one, they hated to dress up, these young ones. They wanted everything they did casual-like including their affairs. Funny kids. He had more fun with their elders whose company he enjoyed except when they became drunk or too personal in their jokes and abusive. Yet he knew it was these old fellows he would miss. They would not understand if he had to explain that the day was too close to last Sunday's tragedy. They would think he was crazy mourning over a stranger's death. How would he make them understand, much less believe that he was mourning over his own . . . yes, it sounded crazy. In any case, he was going to miss their company, particularly those with whom he could compare notes about their ailments. He had fun with them last year.

He liked a certain Mr. H. Torres, who, at 70, had long been retired. Mr. Torres did not take medicine as dispensed in drugstores and prescribed by American and Filipino doctors. He claimed he had never been sick all his life.

"I could have continued working," he said, "but what for? It's time I enjoyed life."

He was a mail carrier when he retired.

The old timers sat apart from the boisterous group of relatively younger Filipinos, in their middle forties or younger, at a corner bar down in the basement, practically ignoring everyone else outside the pale of their tenuous fraternity. They talked among themselves, making no attempt to lower their voices even when a speaker was on the plaftorm and they could hear his voice over the loudspeaker. When someone in their group tried to hush the others, all he got was bellicose grumbling.

"Who wants to hear that guy anyhow?"

"A lot of shit!"

"Crap!"

"It's all the same, every goddamned time: organize, united we rise, divided we fall."

The ailing ones exchanged information, the names of their doctors, advised what medicines to take, except Mr. Torres who didn't have anything to do with doctors. He appeared trim and lean for his seventy years.

"You're too fat," he was telling one of the old men in the group. "Maybe you eat too much fat, too much *adobo* and *patis*.

Sure way to get a stroke."

"What do you eat?"

"You'd be surprised. But no rice, no bread. All lean meats. No pork. Lamb chops okay. But you got to know how to broil 'em. Let me tell you."

And he described the procedure in detail. There was nothing special about his method except that he practically burned the meat to remove all the fat. In and out of the oven. Till the meat was fat-free and reduced to almost half its original size.

"I eat lotsa fruit, fresh vegetables. No canned stuff for me," he continued.

Sol wanted to ask him about arthritis and many hearts beating all over the body painfully, but perhaps some other guy would ask him something like his own symptoms. It was not likely, though. Most of them were drunk already. He was amazed at the amount they drank. If he drank like them, maybe he would enjoy himself more. He would be loud like them and have fun.

"Hail, Philippine Independence!" one old man, with a stoop, shouted, raising his glass, spilling the liquor over himself, but nobody paid attention.

Someone was asking Mr. Torres, "Can you still . . . do it?"

Mr. Torres answered, scratching his crotch, "Man, that thing gets so hard, sometimes I don't know what to do with it."

"You know what you can do."

Everybody laughed.

"No way," Mr. Torres was saying. "If I needed anything at all, it's for this thing, this big trouble, I tell you. Bad for the health, you know."

"Baloney! Keeps your blood pressure normal. Your calory count down. You lose two hundred calories each shot."

The group turned their attention to the only one in the group in a tuxedo, an old veteran, of the original Philippine Scouts, hardly any wrinkle on his clean shaven face, and completely bald.

"And you, what do you do to stay alive?"

"I pray," he said, solemnly, walking away, elegant in his evening attire. He climbed the stairs without holding on to the handrail.

"Don't mind him," someone said, "He's a defrocked chaplain. Twice widowed, he might yet outlive his third wife, a Mexican."

"You know," one had a bright idea, "we should organize a

club of our own. Retired Filipino old timers. We'll have a news sheet, mimeographed, exchange ideas on ailments, join other senior citizen groups fighting for privileges."

"Who's fighting for what?"

"Print a racing form."

"Numbers racket."

"Information on vacation spots that don't cost too much. Our favorite TV programs. Maybe some of our own young doctors would notice us and give their services for free."

"The hell they will. These young doctors are only after the American dollar."

"The American cunt."

"What did he say?"

"Yes, that would be a fine idea. An organization of Philippine senior citizens. What shall we call it?"

"*Bayanihan!*"

"Bull! What do you think we are, folk-dancers?"

"Never mind the name."

"We'll call it Filipino Old Timers, Retired."

"Why not just Filipino Old Timers?"

"Filipino Old Timers, Incorporated. We got to incorporate, right?"

"What for?"

"Better, Philippine Old Timers. Or P.O.T. Pot."

"Jeeesus! Whatta name! Pot. Gone to pot."

"Seriously, Philippine is better than Filipino. Because we got to include the women, don't we?"

"Who wants the women?"

"Mr. Torres. He wants the women."

Mr. Torres waved the idea away with his right hand, spilling a little of the brandy he was holding.

"Mr. Torres will be our President. For life."

"How long is that gonna be?" he asked in a somber voice as he drained his glass. He walked not too steadily towards the stairs. Others followed, some stopping by the bar for another refill. Like what the prescription said.

Sol wanted a soda. Most of the other guys had families of their own. One or two were like him. Alone. Perhaps he should have married. The price of loving was too high. And too painful. He did not wish to dwell on it, but there had been times when he felt that nobody had any right to impose such aloneness on one's self. It was not normal. It was not right. Better perhaps that he had chosen the other way, a continuing involvement with people, enduring the vicissitudes, the pains of separation and betrayal, a gradual dying of the fires of love, passion, lust, whatever, the violence, the wounds. Besides, time helped, it was a salve, a suture, an anesthetic. But he was a coward. He could have found one willing to share her life with his, be the mother of his children. How beautiful they would have looked. Some of the grown up children of these old timers, especially those whose mothers were Caucasian, were beautiful people. The couples had had rough moments, but their marriages survived, such as they were. He could have made it, too. Why not?

He ordered scotch on the rocks. Slowly, he climbed the stairs. He would seek out Mr. Torres in the dance hall. Perhaps he would learn something from him.

The main ballroom was empty except for a few couples waiting for the dance to begin. They walked about or sat on chairs lined against the walls. The sound of their voices carried across the hall like a murmur from a restive audience. It was almost eleven and the band had been playing desultorily all night. Someone on the stage was concluding a speech, maybe the guest of honor.

"*Mabuhay!*" the speaker cried, holding both hands up in what looked like defiant surrender.

The applause was mild, scattered and brief.

The women were dressed in lacy mestiza garments, too tight-fitting and suspiciously new. A few of the American wives and girl friends of the boys wore pantsuits in gaudy colors.

Sol thought he saw Mr. Torres in a noisy group standing close to the bandstand, but he was wrong. He could not understand anything of what was being said, but it was probably exciting to judge by the gestures and mien of the men engaged in the discussion. They kept talking, trying to outshout one another and the band that had started to play again. Still no dancers.

Trumpets. He should have known. There would be no dancing until after the guest of honor and a chosen partner, often the muse of the evening, had opened the dance.

"Ladies and gentlemen, fellow countrymen," the voice of the speaker sounded too loud and harsh, "and now the dance! Which will be opened by the Honorable Consul General of the Philippine Consulate with the beautiful Miss Philippine Independence Day 1968 as his partner!"

It was evident after a few seconds on the floor that his honor was suffering from something like gout or had never learned to dance, or both. Miss Philippine Independence Day was carrying his eminence through the paces of the special waltz number. Her face, close to his, shone with too much mascara that had begun to drip. She kept alternately stepping on, and raising, the hem of her long gown while her distinguished partner, with a silly grin on his face, dragged his feet on the floor.

Sol took a sip from his glass, smiling to himself and thinking, everybody has a sickness.

A few more gray heads among the bald, the thickly pomaded ones, and the long-haired, but no Mr. Torres. Could he have gone home after that exit line about his own mortality?

Sol stopped looking for him. He bowed to those whom he recognized, returned their smiles. Sometimes, even this late in life, the vanity of his younger days surfaced like a trained seal, and he was his old showoff self once again, as he stood more erect than usual, dapper and not so old-looking, his still thick black hair parted near the middle, Robert Taylor in civvies on D-Day, The Sixth of June. But perhaps nobody in that gathering had seen the movie.

Someone had taken a snapshot of a group with a Polaroid camera. As they waited for the film to develop, a few of the women had edged closer, obviously to be among the first to see the picture. When it was finally ready, there was a rush towards the man who held it over their heads, saying, "Careful, it's still wet!"

"Stop pushing."

"Sorry. Let's see."

"Don't hold it like that."

"Let's see. It's my turn."

"You're nice in there."

"You also."

"How much is that?"

A timid, grasshopper-like man in *barong* had asked the question. Sol remembered seeing the man on previous Philippine Independence Day celebrations. He taught elementary Spanish in a southside school which was largely Puerto Rican. But he could not recall his name. He remembered, however, the man's intense pride in everything Filipino. The Filipino could do no wrong in his book. He kept a record of all Filipinos in the States who had made the news media. He argued against those who insisted that some of the persons in his list were not Filipinos, that they only had Filipino-sounding names, that they could be South American or Spanish. He would not have any of that. Doubt in this regard was a form of disloyalty to the country. And look at their pictures, don't they look Filipino even if nothing was said about their country of origin? These were children of Filipino old timers in the States. Who doubts that this quarterback is Filipino? The youngest and fastest reader in the world is Filipino.

Before the night was over, the man was at it again, regaling his audience, inspiring them with his message of Filipino superiority. Sol smiled knowingly, loving the man and pitying him as he fought against those who claimed he could be wrong. Then they started baiting him.

"What about that guy who killed his wife and all their children, six of 'em? He got a Filipino name, no?"

"He's no Filipino. Some other nationality, maybe. But not Filipino, I'm sure."

"How can you be so sure?"

"The newspapers don't say."

"They don't say here, your quarterback is Filipino."

"They say, too."

"What about the youngest heroin addict, a 12-year-old Filipino, ain't he?"

"Oh, no!" the man cried as though he would choke. Then from nowhere, another ineffectual-looking old timer broke into the argument, saying softly, "You're too young most of you to know this. F.D.R. The Roosevelt, he die in arms of Filipino steward in Warm Springs, Georgia," and walked away. Nobody paid him any attention. Maybe most of them didn't hear or care.

In this other group, the women were older. Their eyes lighted up as Sol approached. One of them knew him.

"Oh, how are you, Mr. King?" the old lady beamed. "I've not seen you for some time now. Since last Independence Day. It seems we meet only on this day." Then she began to introduce him to the others.

Sol looked at his glass. It was almost empty.

"We were talking about our favorite TV programs. You watch TV, too, don't you, Mr. King? I told them my favorite is Search for Tomorrow. Most of them like Let's Make a Deal.

44

Do you know these programs, Mr. King?"

"Yes," he said, jiggling the ice cube that was almost melted, wondering how he could walk on at this point without appearing to snub them. "I think I'll have another drink," he said, moving away.

Sol went straight home to listen to his pains.

❦

— *What good that green card do you?*

— *Now I can get better job. I kiss you beautiful green card.*

— *Kiss my hass. What's wrong with dribing a cab. You make good money. Like I do.*

— *Guess I'm tired, that's all. Besides, all I see here are color people. Bet they think I'm color too.*

— *Of course, you har. I look like a white man beside you.*

— *O, quit it! We're Pinoys, we're not color, we're not white. But Jesus! I come to this country to enjoy, you know, blondies, hitting the jackpot, money in the bank, happy happy, but I'm surround by Africa. Oh, I know there's nothing wrong with 'em, but they're too big like they're gonna crush me any time. And I can't breathe. I get my lungs destroy smoking 'em out. Maybe I go to another state.*

— *You're crazy. Where you gonna go? They're everywhere. In the White 'ouse maybe? White 'ouse my dick. One day they're gonna call that place Black 'ouse. I like that. I like 'em black people. They'll be kings of the world, a black world. You know why? They don't die, that's why. I mean they don't die like they get sick. They live porever, that's why they shoot 'em.*

— *They make trouble, that's why.*

— *You know what's wrong with you? You're scare. Like that time I take you to this Pinoy party, lots of heats and so porth, but you don't wanna stay. You're scare of your hown people.*

— *But those are different Pinoy. They're educated, they're rich guys.*

— *Rich guys? Didn't ya see 'em heating with their 'ands,*

46

talking with their mouths pull of pood? Didn't ya see 'em licking their pingers like they gonna heat 'em too?

— *Yes, but . . .*

— *And the girls, their faces like masks, smelling like broads, scratching their be'inds. I know where they hitch too. And some of those guys they're crazy about 'ave wives back 'ome who write 'em sweet letters, I miss you, darling. They pray God keep my 'usband well. And their 'usbands har pucking around.*

— *Ha! You're envy.*

— *Me? Enby? You know why I left 'ome. Don't ya porget that. No more Philippine girl por me. Too much expense. Too many tears. In this country, no problem. You want a woman. You get onc. Por kilo. Bang. Pinish, You porget.*

— *What's to forget?*

— *Besides, those Philippine girls are nuts. 'ave you talk to 'em? They always hask what cha doing 'ere? I can't say just pucking around, they'll scream like I'm raping 'em. If I say I'm a cab driber they make like the talk is pinish unless they wanna ride my cab por pree. So I don't say. I make like there's mystery story. Like I'm Mississippi gambler with lots of money. They see my writs watch, the rings in my pingers. They see the debil in my highs. I can get 'em. But I gotta marry 'em pirst. Who like that?*

— *Guess you're right. But those parties ain't for me. Like I don't belong, like they know I ain't high class. And they use different language with some English words like it's Pilipino with American accent.*

— *'ear! 'ear!*

As soon as Sol received his green card immediately after the war, he knew that for him there was no more going back to the Philippines. He was, legally and in fact, a U.S. Permanent Resident. Again, fate had spoken. Now there was one thing he had to do, master the English language as a way out of the many difficulties that plagued the lives of his countrymen in America. True, his accent would be there always, like his complexion, but a conscious attempt to improve his English was imperative. His mastery of the language was to be part of his survival kit. Read. Read. Listen. He would listen to everything, pay close attention. When he talked he must articulate well without affectation. He had been doing this and had suffered what almost amounted to ridicule from his friends and fellow workers in the munition factory outside Washington. They called him professor. What the hell, they were plain envious, that's what. What do you know, the natives were green with envy.

He was young. He had all the time in the world. *Time was of the important* as he was fond of saying. How strange that even in his mind the ungrammatical structure of this particular thought should strike him as quaint and not too harsh sounding. Cute perhaps, but sincere in the way platitudes were not and serious, the way the rhetoric of lost causes didn't seem to be. Not to him, in any case.

Once long ago as a newcomer in this country, when asked whether he dreamt in English, he was quick to answer, yes, apart from dreams without dialogue. Yet afterwards he was not too sure. Not until he had begun to listen to his own thoughts. Then he knew without doubt that his answer summed up the truth of both his predicament and his intent.

Many years later, that last time out of Washington, he vowed to keep clear of such concerns and involvements that drained him of every ounce of emotional energy and henceforth live it up in words, instead, get drunk with language not only at every opportunity, but to create such opportunities as allowed him to sense in words the heady vintage of his second language. Although the language as the Americans he knew spoke it was a world apart from the language of his favorite American poets, he would, nonetheless, plunge headlong into the mainstream of current speech and writing, breathe into the lungs of his being all the cliches that polluted the air of sensitive purists who wasted time, precious, golden time, watching the pollen count of what was trite and overused to death. He would take in all those cliches and add to them the flavor of strangeness. Why, even his accent wasn't bad, not bad at all. The girls, especially those on the night shift, half asleep most of the time, loved it. When he pronounced their names, like this girl's, named Barbara, she put her covered head on his shoulder and touched his cheek gently with her gloved hand, which smelled of oil. "Say that again," she sighed, and when he did, she practically swooned in his arms in a gesture of complete, absolute surrender.

The language, his accent, not to mention his good looks, would make up the sum total of his personality, his charm. Now he found himself speaking in English to his own countrymen even when they spoke to him in the dialect. Once in a while, when he tried to speak the dialect, he would pause in the middle of a statement, groping for the right word, a turn of phrase that had once been familiar, and revert to English in a strange paraphrase.

Sol decided to attend night school. When he began to make inquiries about going to school nights, some of his friends told him frankly he would be wasting his time. What did he want to be, a politician? Go back to the Philippines and run for senator? His boss had other ideas.

"What you wanna go to school for? You think you earn more? Nah! You gotta be smart here," he said, touching his head with a greasy forefinger. "You don't learn that in no school. Besides, you miss the time anahuff on the night shift."

Instead of getting discouraged, he became determined more than ever to resume his studies. This guy with his illiterate English would be no better than a factory boss all his life unless he became a crooked operator and joined a big time gang. No, he wouldn't listen to him. And what did he care for time anahuff?

The first night school he attended proved to be a mistake. It was an adult class, mostly of aging aliens, who spoke very little English, and attended the class to prepare for U.S. citizenship. He could be their teacher. What he wanted was something else. Regular college night classes.

He applied for admission to a freshman class in English in the extension department of the American University, but he was turned down at first because he didn't have any credentials. He claimed that the high school in the Philippines where he graduated was burned down during the war. All the records were burned with it. But he was willing to do anything to prove that he was eligible for college work. Sign an affidavit. Swear on the Bible. Anything. Did they want to examine him? He was ready.

The admissions official had a baby face and looked amused when Sol said that he was ready to be examined.

"It's the honest truth, professor, I'm a high school graduate. It isn't my fault that I have no credentials. Blame the war." He wanted to say, blame the fucking war, but he was afraid he might be sent up to graduate school for using such language. He was not yet ready for that.

"Let's see. Your case deserves study." Baby face still wore that amused look. He appeared delighted, listening to this young man talking like a book. His blue eyes seemed to say, go on, say some more, I'm listening.

"Some of my teachers were Americans. They're still there. And I'm here. They were good teachers. It was from them that I learned to love English. I've read Edgar Allan Poe, William Cullen Bryant, Henry Wadsworth Longfellow, John Greenleaf Whittier. I know some of their poems by heart. I have won in a declamation contest, interscholastic. I recited Poe's 'The Raven.' Do you want me to recite some . . . ."

"That won't be necessary," the professor said, a pink smile spreading on his cherubic face. "To tell you the truth, I couldn't follow you . . . I mean, I couldn't understand much of what you were saying, at first, that is. But later . . . now, I do get the drift of your speech."

"A speech, sir? Did I sound like I was delivering a speech?"

"Oh, no, no!"

"I'm very strongly moved to ask for your consideration, that's why, sir."

"I know. Perhaps we can admit you as a special student."

"What's so special, sir?"

"Not so special. Special. A special student is allowed to attend a class and pay a minimal fee, but is not entitled to a certificate or degree like regular students in good standing."

"Ah, a visitor."

"Not exactly. Auditor would be more like it."

"Auditor?"

"You know. Audit. To hear. Auditor. Hearer."

"Oh, I thought for a while . . . I mean, we have an auditor general in the Philippines, but that's not it, I guess."

"Oh, no. That's a different auditor."

"In this class I might be allowed to attend, as you say, what do I do? Just sit and listen? I wouldn't be allowed to recite?"

"Of course, you would. You would be a member of the class. Recite when called upon, do the assignments, take examinations, if you wish, and you could have a grade."

"Special. Auditor. The name isn't really that important, is it, sir? I just want to improve my English."

"Your English is fine, it's excellent. Even your accent. After a while, it's fine."

On that fine note, he attended night school. Now he showered twice every day, once on waking up in the morning and again upon arriving home from work. He changed into a clean shirt and a well pressed suit. Well-scrubbed. Spanking clean. Compliments he loved to hear from those who noticed him. He had a natural fresh-from-the-shower look about him. No amount of menial work or hard physical labor, hunger, deprivation, seemed to alter the youngness of his face, the silky texture of his palms so that whenever he shook hands, with girls in particular, they often asked, was he an artist, a pianist maybe, his palms were so soft and he had such beautiful fingers. And he would quite candidly say whatever he was at the time: cab driver, stevedore, laborer, janitor. Surely, they would say, he was joking.

His first class was a disappointment. Grammar. Diagramming.

Rules. He didn't want any of these. All he wanted was to learn how to write correctly and speak well. The rules be hanged.

But he suffered it all. Stoically, he said to himself, wishing someone had heard him and had asked what the word meant. How impressive he would sound in his knowledge, terribly limited such as it was, of etymology. Stoic, from the Greek *Stoikos*, a philosophy of indifference and unfeeling (almost) to either pain or pleasure.

But he was not a stoic. That was the trouble.

The class met three times a week. Sol was present every time. Winter presented problems like transportation. He had no car and waiting at the bus stops in the coldest winter nights, he kept himself from freezing by jumping up and down and swinging his arms about. One night during a blizzard, he stayed home only after he was informed that classes were suspended.

During oral recitation week, he volunteered to speak. He was afraid he might not be called if he simply waited. It was their last meeting for the week.

"What will you talk about?" the instructor asked. He sounded like the actor Edward G. Robinson and looked like him, too.

"Many things," Sol answered confidently, feeling he had prepared for this moment, the moment of truth no less, the hour of unburdening. He was the cynosure of all eyes. There were a few pretty girls in the room and they had fellows waiting for them after class. No matter. He would make them forget their boy friends.

"But you have fifteen minutes only at the most, maybe ten."

"Just stop me, sir, when I've eaten up my time."

He began haltingly, apologizing for his accent and the very personal nature of his talk.

"This is all about me," he began. "I come from the Philippines where I finished high school. It had always been my dream to come to the United States. As you can see I have realized that dream. Perhaps you would want to know whether the reality is anything like the dream. The answer is yes and no. But I won't go into all that. I have only fifteen minutes at the most."

"Never mind the time," seemed to be the meaning of the audible murmur that broke the silence briefly and the look in his classmates' eyes. This gave him added assurance.

"In the Philippines my American teachers taught me to love the works of American poets, but, alas, nobody knows them here. Some recall their names, Longfellow, Poe, Bryant, and the rest, but very few remember their works. And I thought that as soon as I touched American soil, all I had to do was mention 'Evangeline,' 'Hiawatha,' 'The Raven,' 'Annabel Lee,' 'The Death of the Flowers,' 'Rhodora,' and every door would be open to me. Not that doors have been shut in my face because I have tried to quote lines from these poets, but I have been stared at with eyes that seemed to say, 'What a pity that one so young could be so crazy already,' or words to that effect."

There was tittering from girls in the back row. He glanced towards them. Their eyes were applauding him. Maybe they no longer remembered the guys outside waiting for them to be dismissed. Edward G. Robinson's double was doubling with silent laughter somewhere in the rear of the room.

"I should have been discouraged, but I was not. I knew that one day I was going to find an audience receptive to the beauty of the poems I carried with me like a treasure. So I went about my way, throwing around my favorite passages from these poets, waiting for recognition from anybody, any group who would throw back at me a similar bouquet of lovely poetry. But they only threw me surprised glances. Some actually suggested I must be drunk. Oh, yes, I was. I still am. Drunk with words, with the sweet, musical words of the American poets whom I loved, but none of my acquaintances in America knew well enough to understand the nature of my insanity, if insanity, indeed, it is. But tonight, I believe I have found the audience I have been looking for."

The class was in a mild uproar. What had he said? What were they trying to tell him? His time was up? He looked towards the instructor, who was smiling and nodding as he leaned towards a group of students who must be asking him to allow him to keep talking. He had just begun. Finally, he could distinguish some of the things the class was saying.

"Recite the poems!"

"We don't know those poets."

"You don't?" he asked. It was incredible. "Really, you don't? You mean to say you haven't memorized such lines as: 'This is the forest primeval, the murmuring pines and the hemlock . . .'" and he went on and on, leaping from verse to verse and poet to poet by simply saying, "And this from 'Annabel Lee,' . . . and we loved with a love that was more than love, I and my Annabel Lee . . . and the moon never rise but I see the bright eyes of my beautiful Annabel Lee . . .' Or this from the 'Rhodora,' 'If the sages ask thee why, this beauty is wasted on the earth and sky, tell them, dear, that if eyes are made for seeing, then beauty is its own excuse for being.' Don't tell me you haven't memorized these lines."

"No, no. But go on!"

And he went on, like a fool, he thought later, unburdening himself of all beautiful lines he had wanted to hear himself say all of the two, or was it three, years he had been in America.

He regaled them with anecdotes. Once when he told a girl he liked, "Your breath is as sweet as kine that feed in the meadows," straight from 'Evangeline,' the girl refused to see him after she found out that kine meant cows.

Still they kept asking for more. So he went berserk. Soulfully, dramatically, he intoned:

"The melancholy days are here, the saddest of the year,
Of wailing winds and naked woods and meadows brown and
　　　sear,
Heaped in the hollows of the grove, the autumn leaves lie
　　　dead,
They rustle to the eddying gust and to the rabbit's tread."

"And listen to this. My favorite teacher, A Miss O' Malley from Boston, read and reread to us, 'Snowbound' by you know whom . . ."

His classmates looked at one another.

"Well, Miss O'Malley, around Christmas time, did nothing but read from 'Snowbound.' She kept talking to us about snow. We had never seen snow. Our idea of snow was drugstore flakes on a Christmas tree covered with cotton balls or something like in the movies. And she would recite, homesickness in her eyes:

'No cloud above, no earth below,
A universe of sky and snow . . .'

while we sizzled in the classroom.

After class, the only thing his classmates didn't do, which he hoped they would, was ask for his autograph. But perhaps they were afraid he didn't know how to write. A joke, a joke, a joke!

At their subsequent meetings, however, the class reverted to diagrams, and worse, punctuation and spelling, and a record cold spell stayed too long in the Washington area. First, he missed a class, then another. About the end of the term—and thoroughly ashamed of himself—he attended class. He looked around self-consciously, ready with an excuse should someone ask why he had absented himself so long, had he been sick or what? To his surprise and his disappointment, no one seemed to have missed him. The instructor gave them the subject for a theme, due the first meeting after the Christmas break. Subject: My Philosophy of Life.

Now he had a rather strong motive to resume attending class. He was going to show them he could write as well as talk. Could he, though? He had never tried writing. Besides, what was his philosophy of life anyhow? Honesty is the best policy? Cleanliness is next to godliness? That's not a philosophy, that's sanitation. So. What did he believe in?

He believed in Fate. In lives that are extensions of other lives. Like his and Robert Taylor's. That their lives followed a sort of pattern, running parallel but close, so close they touched at certain points ever so lightly but palpably, like pure coincidence—and mystical because unnatural. But this was mere belief, strong as it was, but not philosophy.

He went around, asking at every chance he got, "What's your philosophy of life?" hoping that by listening to others, he would learn how to formulate his own. The guy with whom he often shared the same seat on the bus said, "Philosophy of life? Workers of the world, unite. You have nothing to lose but your change—loose change." The man chuckled, completely pleased with himself.

Others gave out with mottoes he had heard of before and didn't sound like anything nearly close to what he was looking for. He wanted something with an impact. One of those statements that hits you between the eyes, something memorable, a blow below the belt, a kick in the groin, at the least, a tingle. Like what for example?

Like this picture of an old, ragged man, kneeling on the floor beside a sagging bed, saying, God, remember me?

Another picture: of a man in pajamas, unshaven, his eyes still heavy with sleep, talking to himself as he stares at his face in the mirror: "What mistakes are you going to make again today?"

"Life is but an empty dream . . ." Longfellow

"Roses are red, violets are blue
I'm still beautiful, but what happened to you?"
                                        - Anonymous

55

Seriously now, what philosophy? It's better to receive than to give. Any time. Merry Christmas!

There were scribblings in the men's room at the World Trans-Lux in downtown Washington:

See Wanda Supple, 69 4th St. S.W., after 5 pm if you wanna good fuck or a blow job

And right below, in red ink:

For your spiritual needs, Call on JESUS, Address:
Heaven. Open: Night and Day

Obviously written in a different hand, also in red ink, underneath all these was a P.S.: May I call collect? (Signed) John Leland Scrooge.

None of these came close, most of them were just intended to be funny. Could he not, however, extract an essence out of these various texts and pictures and formulate a philosophy of life? Perhaps. But it would not be *his* philosophy of life.

The truth was he had none. That is, nothing that he could spell out like a rule on punctuation marks.

The new year found him without anything written down. His thoughts were as vague and mixed up as ever. Perhaps he would have to tell the instructor frankly that he couldn't do it, he didn't have any philosophy of life, nothing original, exclusively his own. It didn't have to be, though. He could borrow from his favorite poets, but they sounded so sad. Longfellow's "Life is but an empty dream" was more like an elegy for all losers than a philosophy of life.

When classes resumed he didn't show up. The term was almost over. He had paid all the required fees. What did he learn in class anyhow? What a ham, what an ass he could make of himself, that he could be funny like a clown? Shit!

❦

One two
Bato
Three four
Bapor
I love you before
But now no more.

$\mathcal{Y}$

As Sol was about to get in her, she said, wait, pushing him away, are you sure you locked the door? Yes, yes, he said, pressing close and hard. Don't look at me that way, she said. Now, that's better. Easy. Hey, you're rough, you know? Oops! Slipped. Let me. But I warn you, this is my fertile period. Will you stop talking, he said. If I got pregnant . . . Shut up! he said. Just now, all he wanted was get in her. Stop moving, will you? Make up your mind, oops! when I don't move, you say, be lively will ya, shake it up! Now you don't want me to move. Oh, shut up! Okay . . . okay. Now that's great. That's it. That's great. Nice going. Hey, wait, wait, she said, holding him tight, don't move now, hey, you're very good looking, you know, this very second, you're, gosh, you're beautiful! He still wanted to get going, it was pretty good, but this kind of talk, he liked, too, so he slowed down a bit. But hell, they said the same things, in the proper mood, only their accents varied. Okay, I'm handsome, he said, I'm beautiful, but let's go on, shall we? Wait, wait, please, she said, let's make it longer, just now, just this very now, you look like . . . like . . . there's an actor you look like, what's his name? Sol held his breath. Like whom, he asked. She was regarding his face, studying it curiously. Sol's body had grown limp and she felt it. Like whom, tell me, like whom? he kept repeating, his face close to hers, pulling her with him as he fell sidewise. He leaned on his elbow, asking, tell me who. Say who. Who? She was staring at him and she looked so lovely. He drew her close, kissing her deeply. Wow, she said as he released her, wow, that was good, you should've done that first. You know, Sol, you don't even say good morning. You unlock the door, you find me in bed and you take off your clothes, then you want to do it right off like now. And afterwards, you look so solemn on your way to the bathroom. He kissed her again. I'm okay now, he said. Boy, you sure are, she said, pulling him over her, I'm ready, too. Wham! Bam! Over. Now, what were you saying, he asked. She said nothing, her lips pursed, while she kneaded the flesh on his shoulders with both hands. I wanna bite you, she said. You bit me already, he said, look, but tell me, whom did you think I look like. I was only joking, she said. No, you were not, tell me, tell me, whom do I look like? Of course, you look like yourself, silly.

Another dud. But she almost said it. Wouldn't anybody ever say it? They should see the resemblance. Was everybody blind? Or was he the blindest of them all? Couldn't be. But that's how it is. Story of my life.

"Now what. Baby's sulking. I love you, Sol. I love you very much. You're really very good looking. I love the way you talk, including your crazy poems. And you have a sense of humor. Wrong timing, maybe, but funny, funny good. Like the name you've given me. Morningstar. Fantastic. You win the prize, baby. But don't you think this has gone too far, it's become a dreadful habit. Oh, but I should complain. Who's that goddamn woman poet you once quoted to me, your lips twisting so, your eyes all sparklers?"

He knew whom she meant. " 'I know I'm but summer to your heart and not the four full seasons of the year . . .' " he began.

"That's right, that's what I mean, I'm your morning lay. Seriously, darling, why don't we try other hours, ha?"

Sol himself had become self-conscious about the whole arrangement. Everything was timed to the last drop, as he often thought of the affair, bemused and not the least bothered until she began complaining about it even as she insisted she wasn't complaining.

"Don't you realize," she said, "that some neighbors might

find it funny that your car—bet they think it's a fire engine—
that it should always arrive in front of the apartment every seven
o'clock in the morning, right on the dot, the four foul seasons. . .' "

"Full," he corrected her.

"Foul," she repeated. "And leave again on the dot, a quarter
before eight. You beat the sundial for accuracy."

"You exaggerate."

"I do not!"

Morningstar worked nights and it took her an hour by bus
to come home. In the early months of their affair, Sol volunteered
to fetch her from work, but later, he found the arrangement in-
convenient.

"Darling, why do you have to live so far? Why don't you
move nearer your place of work? Good for both of us. Closer
to where I work."

"How long do you think I'd be working in that dump? All
my life? I like this apartment and I hate my job. Besides, it was
your idea. You don't have to fetch me at all. Really."

As time went on, in these affairs, Sol could tell when the
break was starting. The schedules got fouled up. Either the girl
or he (usually it was the girl) began to lose interest. Something
always went wrong. There was always something to argue about.
Making up afterwards was becoming more difficult and, often,
impossible.

Morningstar was patient with him. He delighted her with his
thoughtfulness. At least once a week, there was something for
her from him, a flimsy thing, a stone, depending on what they
were celebrating. When her period came after weeks or a month
overdue, they celebrated their good luck. The trouble was, in
their joy, they went to bed again. Then began another long wait
till her period came. Both of them hated condoms and such.
Cramped their style, threw them out of mood.

There were other occasions for a surprise gift. And there
was always an apt note written in his almost feminine hand.
"Roses are red and you in bed saying to me, not bad, not bad."
Atrocious, really, but Morningstar seemed to like them. She loved
him, she declared, everything about him, his way of mispronoun-
cing words, the awkward but cute phraseology, the way his lips
formed, his eyes shining, the unusual rhythm of his speech. She
was a simple girl herself from a small town in Nebraska, and she
adored this strange brown man with the beautiful face. There
were times when she couldn't tell whether he was joking or not,
but she didn't care. He was fun.

Sol had a name for some of the mornings they shared. This morning was "Complaint Hour."

"Sometimes you embarrass me, darling, especially when you leave the engine of your car going, everything rush rush, shove shove, pant, finish, back to the car."

"I'm afraid it won't start, that's why."

"You don't miss a trick. My efficiency expert."

"I think better than 'Complaint Hour' I should call this, 'With love and sarcasm.' "

"No, darling. Simply, with love."

Sol was always thinking of something funny. As they spent most of their time together in bed while their working hours were different, and sometimes on weekends when he was in no hurry to leave, he invented titles or captions for some of their bedroom scenes.

"Now we're in this movie and the camera is taking our picture. Cut! Caption: 'Body and Sol.' "

Sometimes Morningstar was hysterical. Also hysterical in another sense. Sol taxed her patience. He was, for one thing, a jealous lover. Abnormally so. Very possessive. Often he was sorry about it, his outbursts. He tried to explain, saying it was a matter of cultural difference. What the hell was that? He couldn't say. He had read and heard about it, that's all. It was something he could think about, but there was actually no reason for his jealous rages.

The morning schedule got fouled up now and then. There were difficulties setting it right again, but somehow these were overcome because they were honest with each other. The reasons or causes were usually legitimate, unavoidable. Each believed in the other. Once, however, Sol caught Morningstar in what could have been, indubitably, a lie.

They had not seen each other for a week and Sol was quite eager to go to bed with her. She promised, "Well, tomorrow morning."

"What about tonight?"

"I won't be in tonight."

"Why not?"

"I'm going out . . . with some friends."

"Oh!"

"What do you mean, oh?"

"Nothing. Except that, do you realize we haven't seen each other for a week now?"

"You mean we haven't fucked."

"I didn't say that."

"That's what you meant. That's all you're after."

"You're screaming. You're hurting my ears."

"Who's hurting? You don't know who's hurting."

"What the hell are you talking about?"

"You damn well know what I'm talking about."

"Look, if you don't want to see me anymore, why don't you say so?"

"I didn't say . . ."

"Say it!"

"Now, who's screaming."

"Say it! Damn you, say it!"

"I'm going to hang up."

"You do that."

She hung up. Sol couldn't believe it. Not Morningstar. She had hung up on him. God, it was terrible, but he wanted her. She was right, that's what he wanted. Just about all he wanted. What's wrong with that? She wanted it, too. He dialed her number. For a long time the phone kept ringing. Perhaps she had left. So soon? Sol rushed to his car and the damn thing wouldn't start. But after a while, he was off. Nobody home. It couldn't be. She was in. He waited. Sometimes he thought he heard someone moving about behind the door. Then there was complete silence. He went back to the car and sat behind the wheel, waiting. For what? The scene was familiar, a kind of re-enactment of a particular predicament in which he played the same role again and again, till he was typecast.

After the first affair, the ones that followed were no better than re-runs with one major change, the female lead.

Why couldn't he tire of them before they tired of him? Why couldn't there be a permanent relationship, an eternal wanting? He cherished every moment and feared as much as he anticipated the messy end. He loved company, the loving, the warmth, the glow in everything. Morningstar meant more than a bed companion to him. It could be true that he was too passionate. He had been accused of being too sexy. One girl called him a sex maniac. Of course, they sounded sexy themselves when they called him these names. They liked sex with him. They loved his young strong body. His sex. His sexiness. And he had made a fool of himself, many times over, trying to win them back after it was obvious that they had lost interest in him.

Shamelessly, he crawled back, sometimes literally, begging them to take him again. Horrible scenes. He didn't want to think of them. They haunted him. But worse than those scenes was the terrible wanting, including the mere memory of it. He felt and he acted like an addict suffering from withdrawal symptoms. But if it was sex only that he was after, he could have relieved himself easily, by masturbating or paying a whore. In desperation he had tried both. Net result: Disaster. He would never masturbate again. He jerked off without getting a hard-on as if he had simply pricked himself with a needle to let the blood out. It felt just like it, too. The whore bit was worse. He could not be up to it, thinking of all the men who had mounted her, leaving a goodly portion of their filth in her, and such things as disease and pain, not to mention the disgrace of having to consult a doctor for treatment. There would be nurses there, some of them, most likely, Philippine nurses.

How could it be sex only? He loved the girls who showed love for him, everything about them, their voice, their solicitude, their body, smooth and golden and warm and alive, moving at his touch, rising to meet him, sometimes with a scent like an animal's, but even that was welcome. It was a madness. If this kept up, he would be in a nut house.

Morningstar, where are you, he cried softly every morning when he woke up after a listless night. He had tried seeing her where she worked, but failed. Nobody seemed to know her. Perhaps she didn't work there. He inquired from Personnel. Yes, she worked there. But it would take time to locate her. "Is this an emergency?" God, yes, he wanted to scream, a *very emergency*.

This was the part of his affairs that he dreaded most. A repeat of previous embarrassing, ugly scenes. He would tell himself repeatedly, control, control, but he was beyond help. He had lost control of himself. What did he care? What was life without her? He must get her back at any cost. And he knew what the cost was in self-respect and agony. He also knew that even if he got her back, he would lose her again. The same show. Script unchanged. Repeat performance. Summer re-run.

There were times when he felt like calling up the one man in the world with whom he felt a kinship not too easily explained, much less understood. It did not surprise him to read somewhere in a signed article by a well-known reporter who had covered Hollywood during the golden era of the 30's and the 40's, how Robert Taylor was kicked around by women. First Greta, who gave him the cold shoulder without explanation after what appeared to be a promising relationship during the filming of "Camille." And there was Barbara who, in Bob's own words, treated him as "nothing more than a toy, someone to have around the house like a dog or a cat." Poor Bob! Poor Sol!

At least, Bob had his screen roles. Sol knew them all, most of them, at any rate. He went over them again.

In "Wicked Woman" Bob was a mere spectator to a domestic tragedy that ended in murder. In "Magnificent Obsession," he was a playboy. He married Janet Gaynor in "Small Town Girl." She was drunk during the wedding. Again in "Gorgeous Hussy," he was involved in another messy affair. Bob was a softie, willing victim in many of his roles as flying cadet, intern, lieutenant, and, of course, playboy.

In "A Yank at Oxford," Bob was tough, he handled the coquette he had fallen in love with, the way such women should be treated. Without mercy. Slap 'em around. But this was make-believe. Bob and he were soft. No matter how they blustered about, they were the ones who bled in the end. Each in his own way was no better than "A Cardboard Lover."

That was it. Both of them were cardboard lovers. When Sol wanted Morningstar most, he cried, swearing he would not have anything to do with another woman again. Just so he could have her back. Marry her, if she wanted. He had wanted to marry her, but she always made him feel foolish when he mentioned marriage.

Yet, in spite of the agony he was going through, Sol remained considerate, resisting the temptation of calling her in her apartment in the daytime when she was supposed to be home asleep. But once he reached a point beyond reason or shame, he began calling her up and when he got the busy signal, he knew, at least, that she was home in bed. Now this called for immediate action. He rushed to the apartment and knocked on the door, gently at first. When he received no answer, he knocked louder. Still no answer. He pounded on it with both fists and called to her. He didn't realize what he was doing until he saw the angry faces of the other tenants in the building. One lady shouted at him, "If you don't stop that, young man, I'm going to call the police."

Sol muttered, "I'm sorry," and drove away. He didn't care where he was going. Then he realized he couldn't see very well. His sight was beginning to blur. He was crying. He slackened his speed and parked under a tree. He tried hard to check his tears, biting his lips till he could taste the blood. Now he was sure Morningstar had taken another lover. Morningstar was sleeping with another man. Maybe someone in the same office, the same working hours, on the night shift. They went straight to the man's apartment after work. He had no more doubt about it whatsoever.

Why should he try to win her back, keep hanging on and making a damn fool of himself? No, he just wanted to see her, talk to her. Just once more. One more time. So there would be no uncertainties. Uncertainties? A while back he was thinking, she had, without doubt, taken a lover. Familiar thoughts, the same ghastly pattern . . .

When he finally managed to see her, how changed she was. Not only in her attitude towards him, but in the way she looked. Stunning and cold.

"Are you alone? " he asked, looking around.

"Why, who else did you expect? "

"Your lover, of course. Who else? "

"So. So you know."

"What did you think? "

"You've been spying on me."

Oh, God, the scent coming from her! He rose and walked towards her.

"Oh, no," she said, backing away, "Don't touch me, Solomon King."

A scene from "Johnny Eager" flashed before him like a quick change of slides, but it was enough. He spread out his hands, and panting heavily, he stalked her as she retreated, his face as evil as it could get like Bob's, and Morningstar, looking much more desirable than Lana Turner.

"I'll scream," Morningstar cried out. "One more step and I'm going to scream."

Something was wrong. This was not part of the script. Sol threw himself on the nearest chair, almost missing it and hid his face in his hands. He remained that way for some time, thinking of nothing in particular. Then, quickly, he raised his head.

She was still there, sitting on the far end of the sofa, watching him. For an instant, he thought she had left the room.

"You scared me, Sol," she said.

"It has been a long time," he said. "I've suffered. You don't know how I have suffered."

"Looks like you enjoy suffering, Sol. This is not the first time."

"Who enjoys suffering? "

Morningstar shrugged her shoulders. Sol left his seat and went over to the sofa, but not too close to her.

"Sol, let's talk. I want to be honest with you. I know you're a good man. You're fine. But . . ."

"You don't love me any more."

"I don't know. I didn't say that."

"I love you."

"I know. But listen. I don't want to hurt you. I like you very much, Sol."

Then he was kissing her. After a brief, colorless struggle, she was kissing him back. They made love with their clothes on right on the sofa.

"Damn it," she said afterwards.

"I love you," he said.

"I know. But I thought you knew . . . that's what you said, I have a lover."

"Do you?"

"Let's stop this, shall we? Now we can talk about us."

"What shall we talk about? Oh, I know. That from now on, it shall be like old times again."

"No, Sol, let's just be friends. Now you can prove to me that I've been wrong about you when I said all you want is sex. That isn't all, is it?"

"You have a lover."

"Frankly, yes. Please . . . where are you going? Come back here, Sol."

"You have a new lover."

"I said yes."

"You love him."

"Well . . . Maybe I do. I'm not sure."

"You never loved me."

"You know I did. But all we did—God almighty—for how long, was fuck. That's all we have been to each other. Right? A lay."

"You and your lover . . ."

"Of course."

"Oh, God! "

"What's the matter? "

"You do the same things we do? "

"Come on. Don't be funny. Of course, we do. How else? He's good, he's kind, he's very thoughtful. He also makes me laugh. Not as much as you did perhaps. But we do other things."

"What other things? "

"We take walks. We go to movies. Eat out. And just talk. Sometimes we don't . . . no, we don't at all. Unlike you and me, Sol. Let's face the truth. That's all it has been to us. A physical thing. But sex isn't all. That's what I'm trying to tell you."

Sol was thinking of the times they went out when they could. The long rides. Picnics in summer. Rare times, of course, because of the hours of work each had. But he admitted, too, in his mind, that it was largely sex. There was something in her . . . not only her beauty, her scent, her ways, when she was near, but even the memory of these, turned him on like an aphrodisiac.

"We've had good times also," he said.

"But tell me, have we ever been together without us having sex? "

"What's wrong with that? "

"Oh, you'll never understand."

"I understand all right. You like having sex with this man."

"Of course. Why shouldn't I? And why don't you get yourself another girl? I'm sure it won't be hard for you. You're a very attractive person, you know."

"I don't want any other girl. You, you want this man. You make love to him like you make love to me."

"Naturally."

"You do everything that we have done?"

"Yes."

"You play with him. You go down on him. You . . ."

"Yes, yes, yes! Damn it! If that's what you want to hear. Yes, yes! And maybe more! "

She was so mad, she didn't notice that Sol was crying. He was sobbing. His tears were rolling down his cheeks. His face was beginning to look funny.

"What's the matter, Sol? What happened? Why are you crying? " she asked as she shook his shoulders, forcing him to face her.

He sobbed on.

"Stop it! " Morningstar shouted.

He sobbed louder.

"Good God! " she cried as he broke away from her hold and threw himself on the sofa, half falling, as his body shook with uncontrollable sobbing.

Morningstar gazed down on him, frightened and baffled, unable to speak for a while until the sobbing had subsided into a whimper. Now he was sniffling and blowing his nose.

"But you asked for it," she said.

Sol stood up, picked up his jacket, and walked towards the door.

"Where you going? " she cried, running after him.

Sol paid no attention and kept on walking. He unlocked the

door and he was gone. Morningstar stopped short at the door when she realized her dishevelled look and what she was wearing, but she kept calling after him.

As Sol drove away, he vowed he would never see her again. He would never have an affair again. No more. Not anymore this time. It was much too painful. God help me. Please. Never, never again, he repeated to himself. It's too much. This time, for sure, never again. Never. The word rose a whisper above the purr of the engine. Never. Nevermore. It was the raven's voice this time.

Quote the raven, nevermore, as it sank its claws into his crotch. A good thing, there was nothing there, hardly anything at all.

🦋

— I'm only trying to help you. We should help each other in this country.

— Look who's talking. You the guy who run away when you see an old Pinoy approach you. You tell me that yourself. You can't deny.

— That's different. Most of these o.t.'s are bums.

— Ina couple more years, you'd be one of 'em.

— Not me. I save. I make no monkey business. When I retire I'll have everything I need.

— Except friends.

— Who need friends. Besides, I got friends.

— That's what you think. You're gonna lose one now. These guys you're scare are our countrymen.

— Who told you I'm scare? I just avoid 'em, that's all. Some of 'em give me bad time, like I'm a sucker.

— You look like one, that's why. But don't you see, these old guys are lonely.

— Lonely, my balls! After the soft talk come the soft touch, the cry story.

— How I pity you. . . .Because you should've experience the other vice versa. Like I have. They take you to their homes, feed you till you burp. Especially those Pinoys who don't have no contact with other Pinoys. They show you off to their American wife like lost brother. Like they never get a chance to speak the dialect for years and they just keep talking, never mind the wife who don't understand. And when it's time for you to leave, you know you aren't going to see each other no more. Their eyes shine like they're crying. . . .

— I seen tearful fellow myself, but I think he got sore eyes. He should've been ina hospital.

— Have you been to their homes? The walls, they're cover with Philippine things. They're always shoving albums to you. Some of 'em even got the map of Philippines embroidered somewheres. But what's the use, my smart aleck **paisano**, you won't recognize loneliness even it's serve to you on a bamboo tray. . . .

Through the window curtain, Alipio saw two women, one seemed twice as large as the other. In their summer dresses, they looked like the country girls he knew back home in the Ilocos, who went around peddling rice cakes. The slim one could have passed for Seniang's sister as he remembered her in the pictures his wife kept. Before Seniang's death, they had arranged for her coming to San Francisco, filing all the required petition papers to facilitate the approval of her visa. She was always "almost ready, all the papers have been signed," but she never showed up. His wife had been ailing and when she died, he thought that, at least, it would hasten her sister's coming. The wire he had sent informing her of Seniang's death was not returned nor acknowledged.

The knocking on the door was gentle. A little hard of hearing, Alipio was not sure it was distinctly a knocking on wood that sounded different from the little noises that sometimes hummed in his ears in the daytime. It was not yet noon, but it must be warm outside in all that sunshine otherwise those two women would be wearing warm clothes. There were summer days in San Francisco that were cold like winter in the mid-West.

He limped painfully towards the door. Until last month, he

70

wore crutches. The entire year before that, he was bed-ridden, but he had to force himself to walk about in the house after coming from the hospital. After Seniang's death, everything had gone to pieces. It was one bust after another, he complained to the few friends who came to visit him.

"Seniang was my good luck. When God decided to take her, I had nothing but bad luck," he said.

Not long after Seniang's death, he was in a car accident. For about a year, he was in the hospital. The doctors were not sure he was going to walk again. He told them it was God's wish. As it was he was thankful he was still alive. It was a horrible accident.

The case dragged on in court. His lawyer didn't seem too good about accidents like his. He was an expert immigration lawyer, but he was a friend. As it turned out, Alipio lost the full privileges coming to him in another two years if he had not been hospitalized and had continued working until his retirement.

However, he was well provided. He didn't spend a cent of his own money for doctor and medicine and hospitalization bills. Now there was the prospect of a few thousand dollars coming as compensation. After deducting his lawyer's fees it would still be something to live on. There was social security, partial retirement pension. It was not bad. He could walk a little now although he still limped and had to move about with care.

When he opened the door, the fat woman said, "Mr. Palma? Alipio Palma? "

"Yes," he said. "Come in, come on in." He had not talked to anyone the entire week. His telephone had not rung all that time. The little noises in his ears had somehow kept him company. Radio and television sounds lulled him to sleep.

The thin one was completely out of sight as she stood behind the big one who was doing the talking. "I'm sorry, I should have phoned you first, but we were in a hurry."

"The house a mess," Alipio said truthfully. He remembered seeing two women on the porch. There was another one, who looked like Seniang's sister. Had he been imagining things? Then the thin one materialized, close behind the other, who walked in with the assurance of a social worker, about to do him a favor.

"Sit down," Alipio said, passing his hand over his face, a mannerism which Seniang hated. Like you have a hangover, she chided him, and you can't see straight.

There was a TV set in the small living room crowded with an assortment of chairs and tables. There was an aquarium on the mantelpiece of a fake fireplace. A lighted bulb inside the tank showed many colored fish swimming about in a haze of fish food. Some of it lay scattered on the edge of the mantelpiece. The carpet beneath it was sodden and dirty. The little fish swimming about in the lighted water seemed to be the only sign of life in the room where everything was old, including, no doubt, the magazines and tabloids scattered just about everywhere.

Alipio led the two women through the dining room, past a huge rectangular table in the center. It was bare except for a vase of plastic flowers as centerpiece.

"Sorry to bother you like this," the fat one said as she plunked herself down on the nearest chair, which sagged to the floor under her weight. The thin one chose the near end of the sofa that faced the TV set.

"I was just preparing my lunch. I know it's quite early, but I had nothing else to do," Alipio said, pushing down with both hands the seat of the cushioned chair near a movable partition, which separated the living room from the dining room. "I'm not too well yet," he added as he finally made it.

"I hope we're not really bothering you," the fat one said. The other had not said a word. She looked pale and sick. Maybe she was hungry or cold.

"How is it outside? " Alipio asked. "I have not been out all day." Whenever he felt like it, he dragged a chair to the porch and sat there, watching the construction going on across the street and smiling at the people passing by. He stayed on until it felt chilly.

"It's fine. It's fine outside. Just like Baguio."

"You know Baguio? I was born near there."

"We're sisters," the fat one said.

Alipio was thinking, won't the other one speak at all?

"I'm Mrs. Antonieta Zafra, the wife of Carlito. I believe you know him. He says you're friends. In Salinas back in the thirties. He used to be a cook at the Marina."

"Carlito, yes, yes, Carlito Zafra. We bummed together. We come from Ilocos. Where you from? "

"Aklan. My sister and I speak Cebuano."

"She speak? You don't speak Iloco."

"Not much. Carlito and I talk in English. Except when he's real mad, like when his cock don't fight or when he lose, then he speaks Iloco. Cuss words. I've learned them. Some."

"Yes. Carlito. He love cockfighting. How's he?"

"Retired like you. We're now in Fresno. On a farm. He raises chickens and hogs. I do some sewing in town whenever I can. My sister here is Monica. She's older than me. Never been married."

Monica smiled at the old man, her face in anguish, as if near to tears.

"Carlito. He got some fighting cocks, I bet."

"Not any more. But he talks a lot about cockfighting. But nobody, not even the Pinoys and the Latin Americanos around are interested in it." Mrs. Zafra appeared pleased at the state of things on the home front.

"I remember. He once promoted a cockfight. Everything was ready, but the roosters wouldn't fight. Poor Carlito, he did everything to make 'em fight like having them peck at each other's necks, and so forth. They were so tame. Only thing they didn't do was embrace." Alipio laughed showing a set of perfectly white and even teeth, obviously dentures.

"He hasn't told me about that; I'll remind him."

"Do that. Where's he? Why isn't he with you? "

"We didn't know we'd find you here. While visiting some friends this morning, we learned you live here." Mrs. Zafra was beaming on him.

"I've always lived here, but I got few friends now. So you're Mrs. Carlito. I thought he's dead already. I never hear from him. We're old now. We're old already when we got our citizenship papers right after Japanese surrender. So you and him. Good for Carlito."

"I heard about your accident."

"After Seniang died. She was not yet sixty, but she had this heart trouble. I took care of her." Alipio seemed to have forgotten his visitors. He sat there staring at the fish in the aquarium, his ears perked as though waiting for some sound, like the breaking of the surf not far away, or the TV set suddenly turned on.

The sisters looked at each other. Monica was fidgeting, her eyes seemed to say, let's go, let's get out of here.

"Did you hear that? " the old man said.

Monica turned to her sister, her eyes wild with fright. Mrs. Zafra leaned forward, leaning with one hand on the sofa where Alipio sat, and asked gently, "Hear what? "

"The waves. They're just outside, you know. The breakers have a nice sound like at home in the Philippines. We lived near the sea. Across that water is the Philippines, I always tell Seniang, we're not far from home."

"But you're alone. It's not good to be alone," Mrs. Zafra said.

"At night I hear better. I can see the Pacific Ocean from my bedroom. It sends me to sleep. I sleep soundly like I got no debts. I can sleep all day, too, but that's bad. So I walk. I walk much before. I go out there. I let the breakers touch me. It's nice the touch. Seniang always scold me, she says I'll be catching cold, but I don't catch cold, she catch the cold all the time."

"You must miss her," Mrs. Zafra said. Monica was staring at the hands on her lap while her sister talked. Her skin was transparent and the veins showed on the back of her hands like trapped eels.

"I take care of Seniang. I work all day and leave her here alone. When I come, she's smiling. She's wearing my jacket and my slippers. Like an Igorot. You look funny, I says, why do you wear my things? She chuckles, you keep me warm all day, she says. We have no baby. If we have a baby . . ."

"I think you and Carlito have the same fate. We have no baby also."

"God dictates," Alipio said, making an effort to stand. Monica, in a miraculous surge of power, rushed to him and helped him up. She seemed astonished and embarrassed at what she had done.

"Thank you," said Alipio. "I have crutches, but I don't want no crutches. They tickle me." He watched Monica go back to her seat.

"It must be pretty hard alone," Mrs. Zafra said.

"God helps," Alipio said, walking towards the kitchen as if expecting to find the Almighty there.

Mrs. Zafra followed him. "What are you preparing? " she asked.

"Let's have lunch," he said. "I'm hungry. Aren't you? "

"We'll help you," Mrs. Zafra said, turning back to where Monica sat staring at her hands again and listening perhaps for the sound of the sea. She did not notice nor hear her sister when she called, "Monica!"

The second time, she heard her. Monica stood up and went to the kitchen.

"There's nothing to prepare," Alipio was saying, as he opened the refrigerator. "What you want to eat? Me, I don't eat bread, so I got no bread. I eat rice. I was just opening a can of sardines when you come. I like sardines with lots of tomato sauce and hot rice."

"Don't you cook the sardines? " Mrs. Zafra asked. "Monica will cook it for you if you want."

"No! If you cook sardines, it taste bad. Better uncooked. Besides, on top of the hot rice, it gets cooked. You chop onions. Raw not cooked. You like it? "

"Monica loves raw onions, don't you, Sis? "

74

"Yes," Monica said in a voice so low Alipio couldn't have heard her.

"Your sister, is she well? " Alipio asked, glancing towards Monica.

Mrs. Zafra gave her sister an angry look.

"I'm okay," Monica said, a bit louder this time.

"She's not sick," Mrs. Zafra said, "but she's shy. Her own shadow frightens her. I tell you, this sister of mine, she got problems."

"Oh? " Alipio exclaimed. He had been listening quite attentively.

"I eat onions," Monica said. "Sardines, too, I like."

Her sister smiled. "What do you say, I run out for some groceries," she said, going back to the living room to get her bag.

"Thanks. But no need for you to do that. I got lots of food, canned food. Only thing I haven't got is bread," Alipio said.

"I eat rice, too," Monica said.

Alipio had reached up to open the cabinet. It was stacked full of canned food: corned beef, pork and beans, vienna sausage, tuna, crab meat, shrimp, chow mein, imitation noodles, and, of course, sardines, in green and yellow labels.

"The yellow ones with mustard sauce, not tomato," he explained.

"All I need is a cup of coffee," Mrs. Zafra said, throwing her handbag back on the chair in the living room.

Alipio opened two drawers near the refrigerator. "Look," he said as Mrs. Zafra came running back to the kitchen. "I got more food to last me . . . a long time."

The sisters gaped at the bags of rice, macaroni, spaghetti sticks, sugar, dried shrimps wrapped in cellophane, bottles of soy sauce and fish sauce, vinegar, ketchup, instant coffee, and more cans of sardines.

The sight of all that foodstuff seemed to have enlivened the old man. After all, it was his main sustenance, source of energy and health. "Now look here," he said, turning briskly now to the refrigerator, which he opened. With a jerk he pulled open a large freezer, crammed full of meats. "Mostly lamb chops," he said, adding, "I like lamb chops."

"Carlito, he hates lamb chops," Mrs. Zafra said.

"I like lamb chops," Monica said, still wild-eyed, but now with a bit of color tinting her cheeks. "Why do you have so much? " she asked.

Alipio looked at her before answering. He thought she looked younger than her married sister. "You see," he said, "I read the papers for bargain sales. I can still drive the car when I feel all right. It's only now my leg's bothering me. So. I buy all I can. Save me many trips."

Later they sat around the enormous table in the dining room. Monica shared half a plate of the boiled rice topped with a sardine with Alipio. He showed her how to place the sardine on top, pressing it a little and pouring spoonfuls of the tomato sauce over it.

Mrs. Zafra had coffee and settled for a small can of vienna sausage and a little rice. She sipped her coffee meditatively.

"This is good coffee," she said. "I remember how we used to hoard Hills Bros. coffee at . . . at the college. The sisters were quite selfish about it."

"Antonieta was a nun, a sister of mercy," Monica said.

"What?" Alipio exclaimed, pointing a finger at her for no apparent reason, an involuntary gesture of surprise.

"Yes, I was," Mrs. Zafra admitted. "When I married, I had been out of the order for more than a year, yes, in California, at St. Mary's."

"You didn't . . . " Alipio began.

"Of course not," she interrupted him. "If you mean did I leave the order to marry Carlito. Oh, no. He was already an old man."

"I see. We used to joke him because he didn't like the girls too much. He prefer the cocks." The memory delighted him so much, he reared his head up as he laughed, covering his mouth hastily, but too late. Some of the tomato-soaked grains of rice had already spilled out on his plate and the table in front of him.

Monica looked pleased as she gathered carefully some of the grains on the table.

"He hasn't changed," Mrs. Zafra said vaguely. "It was me who wanted to marry him."

"You? After being a nun, you wanted to marry . . . Carlito? But why Carlito?" Alipio seemed to have forgotten for the moment that he was still eating. The steam from the rice passed across his face, touching it. He was staring at Mrs. Zafra as he breathed in the aroma without savoring it.

"It's a long story," Mrs. Zafra said. She stabbed a chunky sausage and brought it to her mouth. She looked pensive as she chewed on it.

"When did this happen?"

"Five, six years ago. Six years ago, almost."

"That long?"

"She had to marry him," Monica said blandly.

"What?" Alipio said, visibly disturbed. There was the sound of dentures grating in his mouth. He passed a hand over his face. "Carlito done that to you?"

The coffee spilled a little as Mrs. Zafra put the cup down. "Why, no," she said. "What are you thinking of?"

Before he could answer, Monica spoke in the same tone of voice, low, unexcited, saying, "He thinks Carlito got you pregnant, that's what."

"Carlito?" She turned to Monica in disbelief. "Why, Alipio knows Carlito," she said.

Monica shrugged her shoulders. "Why don't you tell him why," she said.

"It's a long story, but I'll make it short," she began. She took a sip from her cup and continued, "After leaving the order, I couldn't find a job. I was interested in social work, but I didn't know anybody who could help me."

As she paused, Alipio said, "What the heck does Carlito know about social work?"

"Let me continue," Mrs. Zafra said.

She still had a little money, from home, and she was not too worried about being jobless. But there was the question of her status as an alien. Once out of the order, she was no longer entitled to stay in the country, let alone get employment. The immigration office began to hound her, as it did other Filipinos in the same predicament. They were a pitiful lot. Some hid in the apartments of friends like criminals running away from the law. Of course, they were law breakers. Those who had transportation money returned home, which they hated to do. At home they would be forced to invent lies as to why they had come back so soon. They were defeated souls, insecure, and no longer fit for anything. They had to learn how to live with the stigma of failure in a foreign land all their lives. Some lost their minds and had to be committed to insane asylums. Others became neurotic, anti-social, depressed in mind and spirit. Or parasites. Some must have turned to crime. Or just folded up, in a manner of speaking. It was a nightmare. She didn't want to go back to the Philippines. Just when she seemed to have reached the breaking point, she recalled incidents in which women in her situation married American citizens and, automatically, became entitled to permanent residency with an option to become U.S. citizens after five years. At first, she thought the idea was hideous, unspeakable. Other foreign women in a similar situation could do it perhaps, but not

Philippine girls. But what was so special about Philippine girls? Nothing really, but their upbringing was such that to place themselves in a situation where they had to tell a man that they wanted to marry him for convenience was degrading, an unbearable shame. A form of self-destruction. Mortal sin! Better repatriation. A thousand times.

When an immigration officer finally caught up with her, he proved to be very understanding and quite a gentleman. He was young, maybe of Italian descent, and looked like a star salesman for a well-known company in the islands that dealt in farm equipment. Yet he was firm.

"I'm giving you one week," he said. "You have already overstayed by several months. If, in one week's time, you haven't yet left, I shall have to send you to jail, prior to deportation proceedings."

She cried, oh, how she cried. She wished she had not left the order, no, not really. She had no regrets about leaving up to this point. Life in the convent had turned sour on her. She despised the sisters and the system, which she found tyrannical, inhuman. In her own way, she had a long series of talks with God and God had approved of the step she had taken. She was not going back to the order. Even if she did, she would not be taken back. To jail then?

But why not marry an American citizen? In one week's time? How? Accost the first likely man and say, "You look like an American citizen. If you are, will you marry me? I want to remain in this country."

All week she talked to God. It was the same God she had worshipped and feared all her life. Now they were palsy walsy, on the best of terms. As she brooded over her misfortune, He brooded with her, sympathized with her, and finally advised her to go look for an elderly Filipino, who was an American citizen, and tell him the truth of the matter. Tell him that if he wished, it could be a marriage in name only. If he wished . . . Otherwise . . . Meanwhile He would look the other way.

How she found Carlito Zafra was another story, a much longer story, more confused. It was like a miracle. Her friend God could not have sent her to a better instrument to satisfy her need. That was not expressed well, but amounted to that, a need. Carlito was an instrument necessary for her good. And, as it turned out, a not too unwilling instrument.

"We were married the day before the week was over," Mrs. Zafra said. "And I've been in this country ever since. And no regrets."

They lived well and simply, a country life. True, they were childless, but both of them were helping relatives in the Philippines, sending them money, goods.

"Lately, however, some of the goods we've been sending do not arrive intact. Do you know, some of the good quality material we send never reach my relatives. It's frustrating."

"We got lots of thieves between here and there," Alipio said, but his mind seemed to be on something else.

"And I was able to send for Monica. From the snapshots she sent us, she seemed to be getting thinner and thinner, teaching in the barrio, and she wanted so much to come here."

"Seniang was like you also. I thank God for her," Alipio told Mrs. Zafra in such a low voice he could hardly be heard.

The sisters pretended they didn't know, but they knew. They knew practically everything about him. Alipio seemed pensive and eager to talk so they listened attentively.

"She went to where I was staying and said, without any hesitation, marry me and I'll take care of you. She was thin then and I thought what she said was funny, the others had been matching us, you know, but I was not really interested. I believe marriage means children. And if you cannot produce children, why get married? Besides, I had ugly experiences, bad moments. When I first arrived in the States, here in Frisco, I was young and there were lots of blondies hanging around on Kearny Street. It was easy. But I wanted a family and they didn't. None of 'em. So what the heck, I said."

Alipio realized that Seniang was not joking. She had to get married to an American citizen otherwise she would be deported. At that time, Alipio was beginning to feel the disadvantages of living alone. There was too much time on his hands. How he hated himself for some of the things he did. He believed that if he were married, he would be more sensible with his time and his money. He would be happier and live longer. So when Seniang showed that she was serious, he agreed to marry her. But it was not to be in name only. He wanted a woman. He liked her so much he would have proposed himself had he suspected he had a chance. She was hard working, decent, and, in those days, rather slim.

"Like Monica," he said.

"Oh, I'm thin," Monica protested, blushing deeply. "I'm all bones."

"Monica is my only sister. We have no brother," Mrs. Zafra said, adding more items in her sister's vita.

"Look! " Monica said, "I finished everything on my plate. I haven't tasted sardines for a long time now. They taste so good, the way you eat them. I'm afraid I've eaten up your lunch. This is my first full meal. And I thought I've lost my appetite already."

Her words came out in a rush. It seemed she didn't want to stop and paused only because she didn't know what else to say. But she moved about, gaily and at ease, perfectly at home. Alipio watched her with a bemused look in his face as she gathered the dishes and brought them to the kitchen sink. When Alipio heard the water running, he stood up, without much effort this time, and walked to her, saying, "Don't bother. I got all the time to do that. You got to leave me something to do. Come, perhaps your sister wants another cup of coffee."

Mrs. Zafra had not moved from her seat. She was watching the two argue about the dishes. When she heard Alipio mention coffee, she said, "No, no more, thanks. I've drunk enough to keep me awake all week."

The two returned to the table after a while.

"Well, I'm going to wash them myself, later," Monica said as she took her seat.

"You're an excellent host, Alipio," Mrs. Zafra commended him, her tone sounding like a reading from a citation on a certificate of merit or something. "And to two complete strangers at that. You're a good man," she continued, the citation-sounding tone still in her voice.

"But you're not strangers. Carlito is my friend. We were young together in the States. And that's something, you know. There are lots like us here. Old timers, o.t.'s, they call us. Permanent residents. U.S. citizens. We all gonna be buried here." He appeared to be thinking deeply as he added, "But what's wrong about that?"

The sisters ignored the question. The old man was talking to himself.

"What is wrong is to be dishonest. Earn a living with both hands, not afraid any kind of work. No other way. Everything for convenience, why not? That's frankly honest. No pretend. Love comes in the afterwards. When it comes. If it comes."

Mrs. Zafra chuckled, saying, "Ah, you're a romantic, Alipio. I must ask Carlito about you. You seem to know so much about him. I bet you were quite a . . . " she paused because what she wanted to say was "rooster," but she did not want to give the impression of over familiarity.

But Alipio interrupted her, saying, "Ask him, he will say, yes, I'm a romantic." His voice had a vibrance that was a surprise and a revelation to the visitors. He gestured as he talked, puckering his mouth every now and then, obviously to keep his dentures from slipping out. "What do you think? We were young, why not? We wowed 'em with our gallantry, with our cooking. Boy, those dames never seen anything like us. Also, we were fools, most of us, anyway. Fools on fire! "

Mrs. Zafra clapped her hands. Monica was smiling.

"Ah, but that fire is gone. Only the fool's left now," Alipio said, weakly. His voice was low and he looked tired as he passed both hands across his face. Then he lifted his head. The listening look came back to his face. Now his voice shook as he spoke again.

"Many times I wonder where are the others. Where are you? Speak to me. And I think they're wondering the same, asking the same, so I say, I'm here, your friend Alipio Palma, my leg is broken, the wife she's dead, but I'm okay. Are you okay also? The dead they can hear even they don't answer. The alive don't answer. But I know. I feel. Some okay, some not. They old now, all of us, who were very young. All over the United States. All over the world . . ."

Abruptly, he turned to Mrs. Zafra, saying, "So. You and Carlito. But Carlito he never had fire."

"You can say that again," Mrs. Zafra laughed. "It would have burned him. Can't stand it. Not Carlito. But he's a good man, I can tell you that."

"No question. Dabest," Alipio conceded.

Monica had been silent, but her eyes followed every move Alipio made, straying no farther than the reach of his arms as he gestured to help make clear the intensity of his feeling.

"I'm sure you still got some of that fire," Mrs. Zafra said.

Monica gasped, but recovered quickly. Again a rush of words came from her lips as if they had been there all the time and now her sister had said something that touched off the torrent of words. Her eyes shone as in a fever as she talked.

"I don't know Carlito very well. I've not been with them long, but from what you say, from the way you talk, from what I see, the two of you are different . . ."

"Oh, maybe not," Alipio said, trying to protest, but Monica went on.

"You have strength, Mr. Palma. Strength of character. Strength in your belief in God. I admire that in a man, in a human being. Look at you. Alone. This huge table. Don't you find it too big sometimes?" Monica paused, her eyes fixed on Alipio.

"I don't eat here. I eat in the kitchen," Alipio said.

Mrs. Zafra was going to say something, but she held back. Monica was talking again.

"But it must be hard, that you cannot deny. Living from day to day. Alone. On what? Memories? Cabinets and a refrigerator full of food? I repeat, I admire you, sir. You've found your place. You're home safe. And at peace." She paused again, this time to sweep back the strand of hair that had fallen on her brow.

Alipio had a drugged look. He seemed to have lost the drift of her speech. What was she talking about? Groceries? Baseball? He was going to say, you like baseball also? You like tuna? I have all kinds of fish. Get them at bargain price from Safeway. But, obviously, it was not the proper thing to say.

"Well, I guess, one gets used to anything. Even loneliness," Monica said in a listless, dispirited tone, all the fever in her voice suddenly gone.

"God dictates," Alipio said, feeling he had found his way again and he was now on the right track. What a girl. If she had only a little more flesh. And color.

Monica leaned back on her chair, exhausted. Mrs. Zafra was staring at her in disbelief, in grievous disappointment. What happened, you were going great, what suddenly hit you that you had to stop, give up, defeated, her eyes were asking and Monica shook her head in a gesture that quite clearly said, no, I can't do it, I can't anymore, I give up.

Their eyes kept on talking a deaf-mute dialogue. Mrs. Zafra: Just when everything was going fine, you quit. We've reached this far and you quit. I could have done it my way, directly, honestly. Not that what you were doing was dishonest, you were great, and now look at that dumb expression in your eyes. Monica: I can't. I can't anymore. It's too much.

"How long have you been in the States?" Alipio asked Monica.

"For almost a year now! " Mrs. Zafra screamed and Alipio was visibly shaken, but she didn't care. This was the right moment. She would take it from here whether Monica liked it or not. She was going to do it her way. "How long exactly, let's see. Moni, when did you get your last extension?"

"Extension?" Alipio repeated the word. It had such a familiar ring like "visa" or "social security," it broke into his consciousness like a touch from Seniang's fingers. It was almost intimate. "You mean . . ."

"That's right. She's here as a temporary visitor. As a matter of fact, she came on a tourist visa. Carlito and I sponsored her coming, filed all the papers, and all she had to do was wait another year in the Philippines, but she couldn't wait. She came here as a tourist. Now she's in trouble."

"What trouble?" Alipio asked.

"She has to go back. To the Philippines. She can't stay here any longer."

"I have only two days left," Monica said, her head in her hands. "And I don't want to go back."

Alipio glanced at the wall clock. It was past three. They had been talking for hours. It was visas right from the start. Marriages. The long years and the o.t.'s. Now it was visas again. Were his ears playing a game? They might as well, as they sometimes did, but his eyes surely were not. He could see this woman very plainly, sobbing on the table. She was in great trouble. Visas. Oh, oh! Now he knew what it was all about. His gleaming dentures showed a half smile. He turned to Mrs. Zafra.

"Did you come here . . ." he began, but Mrs. Zafra quickly interrupted him.

"Yes, Alipio. Forgive us. As soon as we arrived, I wanted to tell you without much talk, 'I'll tell you why we're here. I have heard about you. Not only from Carlito, but from other Filipinos who know you, how you're living here in San Francisco alone, a widower, and we heard of the accident, your stay in the hospital, when you came back, everything. Here's my sister, a teacher in the Philippines, never married, worried to death because she's being deported unless something turned up like she could marry a U.S. citizen, like I did, like your first wife Seniang, like many others have done, are doing in this exact moment, who knows? Now look at her, she's good, religious, any arrangement you wish, she'd accept it.' But I didn't have a chance. You welcomed us like old friends, relatives. Later, every time I began to say something, she interrupted me. I was afraid she had changed her mind and then she began to talk, then stopped without finishing what she really wanted to say, why we came to see you, and so forth."

"No, no!" Monica cried, raising her head, her eyes red from weeping, her face wet with tears. "You're such a good man. We couldn't do this to you. We're wrong. We started wrong. We should've been more honest, but I was ashamed, I was afraid! Let's go! Let's go!"

"Where you going?" Alipio asked.

"Anywhere," Monica answered. "Forgive us. Forgive me, Mister. Alipio."

"What's to forgive? Don't go. We have dinner. But first, *merienda*. I take *merienda*. You do also, don't you?"

The sisters exchanged glances, their eyes chattering away.

Alipio was chuckling. He wanted to say, talk of lightning striking same fellow twice, but thought better of it. A bad thing to say. Seniang was not lightning. At times only. Mostly his fault. And this girl Moni? Nice name also. How can she be lightning?

Mrs. Zafra picked up her purse and before anyone could stop her, she was opening the door. "Where's the nearest grocery store around here?" she asked, but like Pilate, she didn't wait for an answer.

"Come back, come here back, we got lotsa food," Alipio called after her, but he might just as well have been calling to the Pacific Ocean.

Mrs. Zafra took her time although the grocery store was only a few blocks away. When she returned, her arms were full of groceries in paper bags. The two met her on the porch.

"*Kumusta*," she asked, speaking for the first time in the dialect as Monica relieved her of her load. The one word question meant much more than "how are you" or "how has it been?"

Alipio replied, as always, in English. "God dictates," he said, his dentures sounding faintly as he smacked his lips, but he was not looking at the foodstuff in the paper bags Monica was carrying. His eyes were on her legs, in the direction she was taking. She knew where the kitchen was, of course. He just wanted to be sure she wouldn't lose her way. Sometimes he went to the bedroom by mistake. Lotsa things happen to men of his age.

𝓥

My father gave me a peseta
To buy a camiseta,
But I didn't buy no camiseta,
I bought chewing gum.

My mother gave me a peso
To buy a queso,
But I didn't buy no queso,
I bought chewing gum.

⚘

Ursula stayed in his apartment every weekend whenever she could make it. She usually did, arriving Friday evening with an armful of books and notebooks and leaving Sunday night. An undergraduate in a community college, she worked part time as a social worker. She had two term papers to write and had barely begun the introduction to the first, which had something to do with the disadvantaged. She was blonde and tiny-boned like a bird and ate very little. Eating bored her, she told Sol, whenever he called her attention to her habit of barely touching the food. "Like you've a vow to fast in my presence," he accused her.

For her part, it amazed her how much Sol could eat. She enjoyed cooking for him whenever she could, inventing recipes or what she could remember of her native cuisine to suit Sol's taste, which was no problem at all because as he put it, "I eat anything that don't bite me first." She could believe him the way he put away what she placed before him. She liked wines, particularly champagne, which Sol kept in his bar, a shelf in a cabinet above the kitchen sink. She knew it was for her only because Sol was not fond of drinking. The first time he was asked by a waitress, "And what would you drink?" he answered, "Water," and thought it odd that the waitress should seem to be slightly annoyed by his answer. He was not trying to be smart. He was new in the country and didn't know the correct answer to many things. Ursula was fond of telling the story to her friends, not because she wanted them to know that her boyfriend was a simple young man from another country, but to prove a point about "cultural differences." She herself was born in Lithuania in a town close to the Baltic Sea of parents who immigrated to the United States, settling in Michigan, where she spent her childhood. On the weekends she missed going to Sol's apartment, it was usually to be present at some birthday or wedding anniversary party in her family or their close friends and relatives from the old home. However, no matter how important her presence at such family reunions was in the traditional sense, a strong force in the community in which her parents lived, she claimed she would never miss being with Sol two consecutive weekends.

"I'd die," she said, a curious accent in her speech.

With eyes closed or without hearing her car drive up the gravelled path back of the apartment, Sol knew when she was around because of the scent she wore, a heavy fragrance of Blue Grass. When she bathed, she rubbed her skin with its oil. Sometimes Sol did it for her. At other times, she rubbed it on Sol. All week the scent stayed, part of the apartment decor. In their first months together, Sol almost went crazy without her as he smelled it on the pillows, the curtains, on the bed sheets, in the paper tissues, on him. Too bad she lived out of town and had no time to be with him on week days.

Later, during the start of the winter term, Ursula was so busy that she read or scribbled notes in bed while she held his hand in hers, shifting it from one part of her body to another, on her thigh, her breasts, in her crotch, saying it made her concentrate better. Her term paper was giving her problems.

"But I'd have more problems—with myself—if I didn't come here," she confided to him.

It was about this time that Sol acquired a problem of his own in the person of a countryman named Artemio Banda, from Rosario, La Union, Philippines.

They met at a drugstore while both of them were waiting for their prescriptions to be filled. Before Sol's was ready, the young fellow had already told him the story of his life.

You pass through a dusty strip of the town of Rosario on the way up to the zigzags of Baguio. His father was a councilor when Artemio left for the States, with Honolulu as port of entry. No, he didn't have to work the pineapple plantation route before he could go to the mainland because although his father was a mere town councilman, his mother was the only daughter of the region's richest couple, who owned most of the fishing boats and the salt fields of Rosario. Artemio had more money than was good for him, he admitted openly. Well, he stayed on in Honolulu because, among other things, Waikiki cast a sensual spell on the young man from La Union. By the time he remembered what he had gone to the United States for, it was October. When he arrived in Los Angeles to enroll in one of the colleges in the area, the enrollment period was practically over. His credentials were not in order. He had not secured an admission form earlier. It was his fault. Moreover, he was not really interested in going to school. The movies and the long-limbed girls with golden hair who walked the streets and lingered in the parks, with hardly anything on, had stronger attraction for him.

At the time of their meeting, he had been in the States ten years in and out of schools on both sides of the Mississippi, staying in each long enough to buy the school's stationery and pennant to mail home to keep his doting grandparents believing that Artemio was, indeed, trying to get an education, and while it was taking him some time, that only proved how difficult genuine education was.

What struck Sol was the smallness of the man. He could have been an undeveloped teenager but for his face, which was old, haggard. He was suffering from recurring stomachaches. Maybe the poor man was not getting enough to eat. Sol pitied him. He wanted to take him to lunch. Artemio looked like a distant cousin, now deceased, who made *bolos* for a living.

"Come over to the house," Sol said, and remembering Ursula, added, "any week-day. Evenings, I'm usually home."

He gave Artemio his address and telephone number. He had already introduced himself, earlier, soon after Artemio gave him his full name and birthplace. To make sure, however, that he didn't forget, he said it again.

Sol quickly forgot about the meeting and the man until one Sunday afternoon, while watching a gruesome wrestling match on TV, the telephone rang and Sol answered it promptly, thinking it was Ursula calling him from Michigan. It was the little man from Rosario, La Union.

"This is Artemio. Artemio Banda. We met at the drugstore," the voice said and there was nothing familiar about it.

But Sol said, "Sure, sure!" without removing his eyes from the wrestling match. One of the wrestlers, with both hands on the rope, was jumping up and down on the chest of the man on the canvas.

"Good, you remember me. I was afraid you had forgotten." His tone was timid. He sounded embarrassed.

"Of course. Ouch! Sorry. I mean, sure, I remember. How are you?"

"Fine. Is your headache all right now?"

"My what? Oh! Yes, yes. Those pills are okay."

"I'm sorry. I know you don't want to be disturbed on weekends, but I happened to be visiting in your neighborhood, so I thought I'd give you a ring, say hello, that's all. I hope I'm not disturbing you."

"Oh, no. No. Sorry, I mean, no, not at all. If you are in the neighborhood, come over."

"Sure?"

"Sure."

"I won't be in the way?"

"Of course not. Why should you be? Come over."

"Thank you."

What a jerk. What a pathetic little jerk. What has a guy like that learned after ten years in America?

The bigger one of the wrestlers had his knee on the other's hairy breast. Wait a minute. Yes, yes. This guy, almost flat on his back, was doing all that jumping a while ago. Now he was getting it, the ape, the son of a . . . a jerk. The other wrestler was pushing his knee hard, harder while with both hands he was twisting the other's arm so that he would be completely flat on his back. But no, he was not about to give up. A close-up of the face in agony, wet with sweat and saliva, but no blood. Sol could hear the bones breaking. Boy, that was loud. There was some other sound he couldn't distinguish. It was a knocking on the door. Now, who could it be? Surely, not the Banda fellow. He had just hung up. And that pounding must have been going on for some time.

It was Banda. Like a lost child, he stood at the door, mumbling, scared like a picture Sol once saw of a straggler surrendering. "Sorry, I'm disturbing you. I shouldn't have . . ."

"Come in! You're not disturbing me. The truth was, I didn't know . . . well, come in." He wanted to ask, where did you call from, but what good was that going to do? He was there. That's all. Maybe he had a portable phone, like a folding walkie-talkie and he had called from the porch.

That day Artemio stayed for dinner. For one who claimed he

had had his dinner, he certainly ate plenty.

"I only have leftovers from last night," Sol said. "But you're welcome to it."

"I'm not hungry. I've already had my dinner."

"Well, I am hungry. I haven't had lunch."

"I'll just sit with you and keep you company. You got a nice apartment in here. It smells good, too."

"Here, try this. It's good."

"I'm not really hungry."

He ate much more than Sol did, who couldn't get over the idea how so puny a man could eat so much. And he had had dinner, according to him.

Artemio Banda never made a move to leave. Well past midnight, Sol was hungry again. "How about a midnight snack?" he asked. "I can fix something quick."

"Oh, no, don't bother. I'm still full. I had two big dinners today."

Sol insisted. The sparring went on. It was the proper thing to do. Why, in the old country . . .

Banda sat down beside him at the kitchen table and ate more than Sol did, while protesting he was already up to here, touching his throat.

Was he going to stay all night? God, I hope not, Sol thought in near panic. But how would he ask him to leave without hurting the man's feelings?

"Well, I guess you'll have to be up early tomorrow, Monday," Sol said.

"Oh, no. I don't work. And I'm not in school now, you see."

Sol was going to say, hell, but I'm a working man and I've had enough of you. Instead, he said, "Well, you live quite far and I have to be up early, you know."

"Do you watch the late late show?"

"Oh, no, I don't. I hate late late shows." And I hate you, I hate your guts. But he didn't have the guts to say so.

Finally, he said, patting Banda on the shoulder, "I think I'm going to bed now. I'm tired. Okay?" And he walked him to the door. In bed Sol could not sleep at once. He was ashamed of himself. Why did he have to do that? But why not? Well, I must have embarrassed him. Now, at least, I'm sure he's not coming back. Sol thought as he fell asleep and had an instant dream of Banda throwing himself in front of a passing truck because he had lost face. It was a messy crash with all that undigested food and ketchup splattered on the asphalt.

90

Two days later while he was eating, the phone rang and as he answered it, he heard a whisper.

"Mr. King?" it said in a voice so small it would have gone through the eye of a needle.

"Yes?"

"This is Artemio. Artemio Banda."

"Oh."

He had hoped he would never hear from him again. Surely, not after practically driving him out of the apartment that night. Now, too, he was addressing him, Mr. King.

"Mr. King. I mean, Sol, how are you?"

"Fine."

"I was just thinking, if you're not doing anything, may I drop in and have another visit with you? It has been weeks . . ."

"No, I'm not working if that's what you mean. But right now I'm eating."

"Oh, I'm sorry. Go right ahead. I'll come later. May I?"

"Sure." What else could he say?

He had not gone back to the table for more than a few minutes when there was a knock on the door. It was Banda. He must have called from the porch or somewhere close by with his portable phone or something again. How else? He could have wings on his feet.

It was more of the same. Sit down. Would you care to have anything? Coffee, maybe? No, no, no, thanks, I'm full. Dessert then? No, thanks, really, I'm full . . . There's apple pie. Or if you prefer, chiffon cake, that's good. No, no . . . go ahead. Please continue eating. I'll wait till you're ready with dessert, then maybe . . .

While Banda waited, Sol said, taste this. And he did. And this. This is good. Then Banda was eating. Not just dessert, but everything. Ravenously.

Sol blamed himself, but he could not simply keep on eating while Banda watched him, his eyes wandering over the viands on the table, following every spoonful, every piece of meat conveyed from plate to mouth, and not say anything. Maybe he was only imagining it, but Sol could hear the man's stomach growling. And the look in those eyes! Where had he seen it before? There was no doubt about it. The man was starved. Perhaps he was no longer receiving money from home. The salt fields in Rosario which his grandparents owned must have been swept into the seas by typhoons, frequent at this time of the year in the islands. Why didn't he work?

"If I were you, I'd look for a job," he said.

"I can't. I have a student visa. So I have to keep enrolling, somehow. Besides, what can I do?"

Sol pitied him. He was so tiny, so weak looking. Maybe he was a freak. But he couldn't tell him, go look for a carnival. That would be cruel.

That was the beginning of what turned out to be much more than a minor problem in Sol's life. When Ursula heard about Banda, she said, "I hope he doesn't come when I'm around. You'll be surprised at what I'm going to do."

"Please don't, whatever it is," Sol begged her.

"You do sound in earnest," Ursula said. "But I'm not going to be silly like you. I'm not going to say, well, you could make a choice, either he's out or I'm out."

"No, no!"

"Of course not, silly! But you have to do something."

During week days, Banda no longer called. Perhaps he was down to his last dime or had sold his infernal talking machine. Now he just showed up, always around meal time.

Sol tried tricks. He decided to eat out. Perhaps he should really eat out more often, but he couldn't stand restaurant food too much, not day after day. Moreover, eating out strained his budget. Ursula bought foodstuff, groceries and such, with her own money.

The trick didn't work. Banda's timing was perfect. He showed up soon after Sol arrived from the restaurant. When he came at such times, Banda waited for what must have been to him an interminable period before asking in a most diffident tone, "Have you had dinner already?"

Ah, I got you! Sol wanted to scream at him. Instead he said, "Yes, I thought I'd eat out this evening and I'm glad I did. Try it. It's good. I think I'm going to eat out more regularly from now on." No hard feelings, my dear countryman, but I cannot afford to keep feeding you.

"Yes? Well, I had supper myself before I came. I thought I'd just drop in; I have nothing to do."

"Help yourself," Sol said as hospitable sounding as ever.

Banda did help himself. To the refrigerator. He kept opening it for just about anything he could put into his mouth: an apple, a slice of pumpkin pie, cold cuts, milk—a full meal!

Sol hung his head in defeat. He might as well tell him to his face, you practically live here, why don't you? Go and get your suitcase and move in. But he knew that would be disastrous. Banda would say, thank you, and accept the invitation.

In his failure to get rid of him, Sol began to be evasive about the situation whenever Ursula asked him about the "sponger." Sometimes she sounded quite sarcastic, asking, "How's hospitality as Filipinos understand it to mean?" in parody of his explanation of how the situation had deteriorated. Sol ignored her, saying it's nothing, he doesn't come too often now. "It's not that important really. You have to read and write a great deal these days, you should not bother your pretty head about an insignificant person like Artemio Banda."

"I wish I could talk to that man," Ursula said. "I'll tell him off, you bet. Just watch me."

Sol had no doubt Ursula was furious and meant every word she said. She must have sensed that it was troubling him more than he would admit, but was helpless to do anything about it. She knew how sensitive he was. He had talked to her often about loneliness, shame and loss of face, the so-called Filipino sense of hospitality. Why, if hospitality were an official game in the Olympics, Filipinos would be the world's perennial gold medalists. However, she was glad, it seemed, that he didn't want her involved in it.

Sooner than she had hoped, Ursula nearly had her wish. One Sunday evening, as she was leaving, Banda showed up. Just as Sol bent over to kiss her after she had started the car, she must have seen (he had no doubt about it) this little brown creature, looking like a waif, standing close by, observing them. As she drove off, she must have known it was Banda and had a hard time restraining herself from turning back.

Sol was angry and he didn't care whether it showed. "Didn't I tell you not to show up on weekends?" he shouted at him. Banda paled visibly and hung his head as Sol walked back to the apartment.

After a while, there was the tiniest knock on the door. Sol cursed himself for not having the heart to ignore it.

"Come in!" he said harshly, leaving the door open.

Banda closed the door and took a chair in front of the TV set.

"I think 'The Untouchables' is on now. May I watch it?"

"What did you say?" Sol asked irritably.

"Or is it the Ed Sullivan show?" Banda said.

"Sorry, Banda, but I'm busy. Why don't you go home and watch whatever . . .."

"I have no TV."

"Didn't I tell you not to come at this time?"

"I'm sorry, but I happened to be in the neighborhood . . .."

"And you thought you'd drop in and say hello."

"Well, yes," Banda answered, adding, "Gee, she smells good." He was sniffing the air.

"What?"

"She's beautiful!"

"Thank you. I'll tell her that."

"Is she . . . is she your . . ."

"She's my girl friend."

"Yes, I know, but . . . I mean, she stays . . ."

"Look, Banda, I want to be alone. Please?" He wanted to add: and mind your own business! Why didn't he begin gorging himself with the food on the stove or emptying the refrigerator? That would have been better than what, obviously, the fellow was now trying to do, meddle in his personal affairs.

"In our country, when a girl . . ." but before Banda could finish what he was going to say, Sol had jumped up from his chair and screamed at him.

"Damn you, Banda! Who do you think you are to tell me . . ." In his anger, he choked. He wanted to strike him. What somehow calmed him down was the look on Banda's face. He seemed on the verge of tears. He had crooked his forefinger and was now biting it. His lips were pale and trembling.

"Oh, good God, I'm sorry," he finally managed to say. "I didn't mean anything bad, believe me. I thought we—you and I—are friends. You've been good to me. I like you. And I like her, too. Very much. I want you together always. I want you married."

"Let me decide on that myself, may I?"

There was no anger in his voice this time. But still, he hated Banda's guts. What was the son of a devil going to do now, Sol asked himself, act as my conscience, judge my morals, make me feel guilty? Or could it be that he actually felt guilty and that was why he wanted to strike him? But why should he feel that way? It was no one else's business but his and Ursula's. He wouldn't even tell her even if she asked, which, doubtless, she would. He would say, Banda stayed a while, ate some leftovers and went home.

This was not far from the truth. Banda ate his fill as usual as though nothing untoward had happened, before leaving that night, saying over and over again, "I'm sorry, I'm truly sorry, I'll never bother you, never," as Sol shut the door and bolted it.

Banda sounded sincerely contrite. Perhaps he had meant well. Somehow Sol felt as he walked back to the living room that was the last time he was going to see Artemio Banda. The fellow was moving to another state, staying on any campus long enough to buy the school's stationery and pennant to send to his grand-parents.

During the Christmas break, Ursula stayed with Sol through Christmas day. She wanted to spend New Year's eve with him, but she had to be home with her family. As it was, she had to give her parents all sorts of excuses about her work and the term papers she was doing. She brought her typewriter and notes and books with her. Sol himself was on vacation. They had hoped to go to the South where it was warmer, but the term paper took much of her time. Sol cooked for her when she was tired. She asked him to massage her neck, rub her back, her entire body.

"That's good, that feels very good," she moaned, often a bit tipsy with wine. She kissed his fingers, licked them wetly or sucked them one by one, sighing contentedly, "Whenever you touch me my flesh jumps towards you. You feel it, don't you?"

"That's right. Your flesh becomes alive. Your smell makes me drunk."

"Are you drunk now?"

"Drunk enough."

And she went wild, clawing at him, kissing him all over, fran-tically tearing their clothes off, crying, "Hurry, hurry, I'm coming . . ."

It was so peaceful afterwards.

"I think I came twice."

"You've been cheating on me," Sol said, pretending to choke her.

"No, don't say that. Even as a joke, please," Ursula reproached him. "But it's true, sometimes I come twice before you do. Oh, sweet, sweet honey darling."

"It's so warm and nice when you're here. Feel how warm, how nicely warm it is with us here like this together alone. And outside the snow's falling. It's grrr . . . grrr . . . out there."

"Let's stay like this always."

"Why not?"

"Oh, let's stop talking about how good it is. Let's just be and talk about something else."

"Like what? Your term paper?"

"Fuck my term paper."

"The sponger?"

"Fuck him!"

"Let's just shut up then and lie here like this. Come closer. That's better."

He watched her close her eyes. In the half-lighted room her

blonde hair shone like first class hemp.

"You're beautiful," he whispered in her ears. "Do you know, I can make love to you again?"

She stirred a little, her hand groping towards him.

"Oh, yes, you can," she breathed huskily, pressing him hard.

"Merry Christmas," he said, touching her.

"Merry Christmas," she whispered, holding him.

When they woke up, it was late afternoon and dark like night.

"Let's not get up," she suggested.

Then they remembered she was going to her parents in a couple of days and they spoke their thoughts aloud. Just when everything seemed perfect, they would think of it: how long she would be away.

"Let's not think of that."

She was getting very little work done, but somehow, in times like this, she did not care. However, she hoped to be able to do something in her parents' home. Every time she thought of leaving she felt so sad she wanted to cry. She was missing him already, that's the truth, not simply a matter of saying.

"What's this spell you've cast upon me, darling?"

Sol had heard other girls say that before. That was what he was to each of them, a spell. And all spells come to an end. On this wintry day, in the warm room, beside this warm creature, he felt a chill.

"I love everything about you, sweetheart," Ursula was saying. "You're a very special person. Are all of you Filipinos special persons?"

"Oh, yes. To very special persons, we are."

"Do you think I'll like it in the Philippines?"

"Who said you're going to the Philippines?"

"Can't you take a joke?"

"I was only joking myself. Come now, Ursula, be a sport."

"Say that again, my name. How beautifully you say it."

"Ursula . . . hey, do you know that Robert Taylor's wife is named Ursula?"

"I thought it was Barbara."

"That was before Ursula."

"Ursula," she repeated, trying to sound like him. "No, no, I can't say it the way you do."

"I like your accent, too, you know."

Sol pretended he wanted something from the refrigerator. He wished he had not mentioned Robert Taylor. Where could she be now? Barbara, his own Barbara, who used to be his, under his spell, the longest, bitterest spell yet.

"What's she, American?" Ursula was asking.

"Who?"

"You said Ursula. Robert Taylor's wife."

"Ursula Thiess."

"Sounds foreign."

"No way to tell."

"That's right. Is she pretty? Is she prettier than me?"

"There's none prettier than you. She's blonde, too, I believe."

"I better be prettier."

"Robert Taylor is a beautiful man."

"He sure is. Have we talked about this before?"

"I'm not sure."

"Maybe we have."

"So you like Bob."

"I like Sol. I think he's better looking than Bob."

"I better be."

"Say, have you ever thought of becoming an actor?"

"No. And stop kidding."

"I'm not. Look at you. Why, you could be a handsome, romantic leading man. Like Robert Taylor."

"What did you say?"

"Aha! He's biting. I said you could be an actor like Robert Taylor.

"Oh." Sol's disappointment was deep, bruising. It was the flaw in an otherwise perfect day, but he asked for it. Couldn't it be, though, that it was what she meant, that he looked like Robert Taylor?

"On second thought, I don't want you to be an actor. I want you all to myself."

"Good enough. Same here."

Ursula tried hard to return to her work. She jotted down notes, started out to write her term paper, but she could not get going. All she wanted to do was cuddle Sol, touch his lips while he talked, listen to his stories. She talked about her parents, of a time when they ran away from some horror in her homeland, but she was too young then to understand or remember what it was all about. Now, of course, she knew what the running was all about, now she understood what all these attempts at nostalgia really meant for the exiles that her parents were, their close friends and relatives, why they felt hurt when she failed to attend their occasional reunions as if she were being unfaithful to them, disloyal to their cause. Sol told her stories of life in the Philippines, but no matter how serious he was in the stories he was telling, she often suspected him of simply trying to be quite entertaining. How she loved to hear him talk. Those lips, sometimes she reached out to touch them. And his eyes, like the lights in the room . . . Her own eyes were aglow. I love you, I love you, they were saying in so many kilowatts beamed on him.

Sol was an excellent story teller and he knew it. Every story he told seemed cut out of the very center of his own life and experience, but this was not true. He was already in this country at the outbreak of the war. Much of it he heard from those who had been there and from letters that came soon after liberation and gradually stopped coming. But it was all true—that, too, he knew.

He told her that shortly before the Americans came to "liberate" the Philippines from the Japanese, there was hardly anything to eat in Manila and in the provinces around it. And when the Americans finally succeeded in driving the Japanese away, the Filipinos, especially the young ones, had stomach ache and diarrhea because they ate too many chocolate bars and canned stuff. When you have been hungry too long and suddenly you find so much to eat, you don't stop to think; gobble, gobble, the abundance couldn't last, you might be dreaming. So you don't care if you get sick or die. You had died many times before. This was a better way to go.

There was great hunger in my province. You see, our government leased a part of the province to the Americans, government land, where our house was, where I was born. And the army fenced this in with barbed wire, Off Limits. A good thing my parents were not there anymore.

"Where are your parents now?"

Dead. Well, inside the barbed wire were mountains of things. Mostly junk. But that junk cost plenty outside this American base. So there was a lot of stealing. The guards had an orgy shooting down the thieves.

"Oh, no!" Ursula hoped he was joking. It couldn't be true. Yet there was something familiar in the picture in her own life, in stories she had heard told in a language her parents spoke.

You better believe it. We held wakes at least once a week in our village alone. Young men, boys, girls so young they stole only what they could eat, nothing else was worth the trouble, older women, old men, grandfathers who admitted openly it was better to die with a full stomach than hungry, then you die with your eyes open. Some of them were shot down and died with their eyes staring stonily at the barbed wires lining a low hung sky. Oh, the howling, the wringing of hands, the loud prayers in these wakes, the drunken fighting among those who gambled all night in the room of the dead, who were later buried at the foot of the hill. And once more the living took up their unfinished task. Of stealing.

"You're making it up. Why would they want to risk their lives? Besides, didn't they consider it wrong?"

Wrong? Who's to say wrong? Or right? No, they didn't think it was wrong. America was too rich. They were cleaning up the base of a clutter of junk. Precious junk they could sell to buy food. It was spoiling in the rain, getting rusty in the sun and the salt from the bay. Odds and ends. Metal parts, engine parts that moved an army, rolled through the land, spreading death on friend and foe. Who's to say wrong? Say survival. A thin way. Sometimes there were canned foods. Coffee. The foodstuff was more dangerous, more risky to steal.

But after years of war, everything was relative. Besides, sometimes it was not that dangerous. It all depended on those young American guards. There were guards who didn't care. They simply looked the other way or turned their back. Or they made sounds to frighten the thieves away. Fired shots in the air. Some of those soldiers were marksmen. They shot at their feet, as the thieves ran with their loot, without hitting them. The villagers were aware of this. They took a chance. A way to live.

A not uncommon sight: a father shooting at his small son with a shotgun, the buckshots dropping all around him as he rolled on the sand, simulating escape. A lesson in survival. Of course, the rehearsal could be fatal, too. The kid could be hurt, but better hurt in practice than in the actual job. Some small kids became experts in evading shots while they rolled on the ground with their bag of loot, right under the barbed wire.

Once outside the barbed wire fence, the boy's family would rush out to meet him from some thick underbrush where they had been hiding while they waited tensely. The mother would crush him to her breast, crying, thank God, thank God, while the others relieved him of the stolen goods. The father would tap him on the head as much as to say, well done, son. Sometimes there would be a scattering of applause from other hidden observers outside the off limits area.

There was a boy, no more than ten, dark and husky, who was so good at it, even the guards must have had some kind of fondness for him. He sang while he gathered whatever he could steal. His voice rose high pitched above the sea breakers, as he picked his way back to his waiting family.

"And what did he sing, if what you're telling me is the truth?" Ursula asked.

And Sol sang the boy's favorite song while Ursula listened laughing through her tears:

You are my sunshine, my only sunshine,
You make me happy when skies are gray,
You'll never know, dear, how much I love you,
Please don't take my sunshine away.

Sol felt remorseful afterwards. Why did he have to tell such stories? She was herself vulnerable. Maybe she knew deep in her heart such things really happened in a war-torn world, but it was easier not to remember, to pretend a mist covered such things, a merciful haze over all the unpleasantness, with bits of sunshine showing through, a trickle of brave sad songs, good times cherished in a child's memory of pastries, hot toddy and warm wool sweaters, smelling of the sun on snow-covered lanes, bonnets and red mittens knitted by loving hands beside a crackling fire in a now-lost Lithuanian coastal town.

Why did he have to talk about all that shooting, the thieving and the wakes? He might have given her the impression that some of his countrymen took to stealing like some Americans to bargain sales. He didn't mean any of that. He should have told her other stories. For instance, the life of the Filipinos in America, their aspirations and delusions, their innocence as enduring as their homesickness, say, like why Banda was the way he was, the root of his sickness. It was a sickness. Why explain? Forget Banda. Ursula understood and felt more deeply than she was willing to admit. That's why she was in social work, reading all those books she brought along with her. Sometimes, though, he wished she wrote more about people with faces and feelings than about cases, supported by statistics and, to him, meaningless charts. But it was none of his business. Besides, what did he know about term papers?

Ursula left for Michigan as soon as the highways were declared safe for travel. According to the weatherman, the radar showed no snowfall in sight within miles of the route she was taking. As usual, as soon as she started the car, Sol bent over to kiss her goodbye. She held on to him, saying, keep warm, darling. You, too, he said as he backed away while she rolled up the window on her side, and just then heard a voice saying, ". . . in our country when a girl . . ." Damn, he muttered as he looked around him nervously, neglecting to watch her this time as she drove around the bend of the road to the west and disappeared quickly behind a complex of other apartments. He wondered, as he always did, when she was coming back. Then he felt how cold it was, standing bareheaded in the wintry evening, and he rushed back to the apartment, closing the door tightly. Yet the chill held on. One of these days she was not coming back. It was bound to happen. In one Robert Taylor movie . . . Sol was shivering. The door had been left open too long.

— *So every night before going to bed, I say goodnight to that Dome of the Empire State Building, my only friend. It's always there even when I can't see it like in winter, but I know it's there.*
— *No wonder, everybody calls you S.S.—Sentimental Susie.*
— *I take it easy now. I used to have visitors in my apartment. I lived near the hospital then, in Brooklyn. Now I don't care if I don't see anybody.*
— *That's what you say, but who don't need company?*
— *My phone bill was something big. I spent more on long distance than on food. You see, I got lonesome nights, especially on my days off, and I'd call friends, nurses, out of state. I stopped that. I better save my money.*
— *You must have plenty now.*
— *Aba, what do you think? With the present dollar-peso exchange, I'd be a rich woman in the Philippines.*
— *What's the exchange rate?*
— *Imagine, si Susan lang, nurse, old maid, with so much money.*
— *Why don't you go back? I know you got relatives out there. Brothers and sisters, right?*
— *I've been helping them. They know I can help them better from here. But I was there two years ago. My brothers showed me the land they now owned thanks to their old maid sister nurse. My sisters, that's another story. They married good-for-nothing men. I don't want to be like them. And they were pretty, too. I'm the ugly duckling.*

— **Talagang** *brain drain, all of us.*

— *Not me. I got no brains. My father, bless his soul, used to lift me over his head when I was a child and sing, My Little Bird up in a Tree or something, and he told everybody I was so little how could I have brains?*

— *But now, look, you got dollars in the bank. Hey, what's the dollar exchange?*

— *I don't know. Six, seven, eight, ten! I'm not sure. The more the better.*

— *I envy you.*

— *What for? You got a doctor husband. What more do you want?*

— *Children.*

— *Count your blessings. It's hell to raise children in this country.*

— *But we're going back.*

— *Lucky you.*

— *But you could go back, too, if you wish.*

— *Like I say, I visit, that's enough.*

— *You mean you want to . . .*

— *Die here? Why not? As Rizal said, "El sitio nada importa." The place never mind.*

— *What do you do when you get sick?*

— *Take aspirin.*

— *I don't mean that kind of sick. I mean real sick.*

— *Go to a hospital. What else?*

— *Who'll visit you?*

— *I don't care. Back home we're swamped with visitors when we get sick and we get a relapse entertaining them. Worse, sometimes, we spread the disease.*

— *That's true, too. But won't you feel so alone being sick and all that?*

— *I can always cry. I've learned how to cry without making any noise. Except when I blow my nose.*

— *Get yourself a man. Fall in love.*

— *I don't believe in love.*

— *I don't believe you.*

— *Believe what you will.*

— *Are these grapes plastic?*

— *You know they are.*

— *But they look so real.*

— *See what I mean?*

$\mathcal{V}$

The old pictures lay scattered on the davenport where Sol had placed them when he had to use the dining table, a clutter in his usually well-kept apartment. He thought he would have time to look them over again now that he had started on his long vacation and had nothing much to do. A viral kind of restlessness was driving him in and out of the apartment. He wanted to go some place, anywhere, yet he never seemed to get started. As soon as he got home, he turned on the stereo, the radio, or the TV. Often he didn't realize that the stereo and the TV were on at the same time until after a while when he discerned an overlapping of voices and sounds, an eerie combination of soft music and a hysteria of bombs lighting up a green and red countryside where sheep and geese ambled by a take away. It was silence that frightened him. Sometimes he left the radio on when he went out so that when he opened the door on his return he would find instant comfort and warmth of a sort from the sound of human speech or song that greeted him, which, of course, gradually faded in the undeniable reality of his aloneness. Whatever, it was company.

He meant to reclassify those pictures in neatly labelled envelopes, plastic containers in various hues, so that he could see through them. Every time he went out, he told himself he would buy plastic envelopes, but he never did. He always forgot.

That was what worried him now. In addition to the pains he felt, particularly nights, that gave him little sleep, he noticed that now he had a tendency to forget what used to be the most familiar things: names, words, scenes, lines from the poems he had been reciting all his life on occasions or for no reason at all, songs. Most of the lyrics of the songs he loved lay buried in graveyards unknown to him. On meeting people he knew quite well, their names escaped him as he tried to address them. They would talk for a while and he would pretend to listen to what they were saying as he tried hard to recall their names. The names, the lyrics and titles of songs, the missing phrase or line from a poem, came later like welcome but unexpected guests, when he was not thinking of them at all.

He stayed out less since the cold had set in. It was warm in his apartment and he could keep busy planning what he was going to do. He was set on taking a trip, but he had not yet decided where. He ought to make an itinerary, a tentative schedule, flexible. That would be best.

Winter came with a rush of hail and sleet. He watched Chicago age suddenly under flakes of snow that clung on buildings and trees in the parks, everywhere. Chicago, you are dying, too, he told the skies.

Perhaps the world was coming to an end. What was he worried about? He was taking the entire human race with him.

"Great, wide, beautiful, wonderful world," he intoned and paused. He could not remember the rest. Oh, yes, the second line ended with the phrase "around you curled," but he could not recall the words that preceded it. And he used to know this poem by heart.

It was too beautiful a world to die. Great happenings were taking place. The men had landed on the moon. It didn't excite him, however, as he watched them. Astronaut Armstrong's words sounded false, memorized, a ghost writer somewhere on earth was congratulating himself as he listened. What thrilled Sol was the expectation of disaster: the moon surface opening under to swallow them, the lunar module failing to take off, or on the way back, somehow their spacecraft failing to break its lunar orbit in its rush to the earth through that narrow space the sensitive instruments from the earth had pinpointed. The idea of a spacecraft with the astronauts inside, in a perpetual orbit around the moon, chilled him. What a way to go. As if the way mattered. It was the waiting. Which of the four seasons was it going to be? Again, did it matter? Each season was tinged with its own color of death. Except in summer and spring, death did not come incognito. He appeared on the scene like an ambitious actor, seeking the limelight shamelessly, upstaging the late sunsets and the blossoming rose gardens.

Soon after Robert Taylor, Judy Garland went, a hag at forty-seven. Sol watched a rerun of the "Wizard of Oz," in which Judy, young and innocent, sang "Over the Rainbow" as she pressed her pretty head on the furry-faced animals around her. Television could be very cruel, Sol realized, choking back his tears. In the fall, his favorite person because he liked the way he spoke and looked, like one of the venerable uncles of his childhood, died, too. But Senator Dirksen had lived a full life.

There was no beating Mister Death. Have all your heart transplants, the time comes in its season. Knowing that, Sol was resigned, or so he said. He had no fear of death actually. Didn't he, really? It was the waiting and not knowing what to do. Or how to forget that the hour was soon. Just let it come. He was beginning to forget everything else, his memory was failing him, but this thought had taken root in his mind and would not allow for anything else. What was he to do? See a doctor again? What could he say to Sol that he had not said yet? Nothing, nothing.

Once, Sol actually got going. As he was driving through the Freeway towards New York, he realized that the traffic was heavier than he had expected. He had a snack at one of the glass houses past the Indiana Turnpike and, driving on, observing the minimum speed, he found himself in the thick of a traffic jam, with all the cars forced to a crawling pace. Then he remembered it was a weekend holiday. He should have chosen another time, but it was too late now. Besides, he was enjoying the ride. He could without trouble make an exit anywhere along the Freeway should he decide to spend the night elsewhere and not proceed to New York. The more he thought of New York, the less interested he was in going there. Who were still in that city among his friends? When he consulted the old personal directories, full of names and addresses and telephone numbers, which he had collected through the years, some of the names didn't mean anything to him. The few that did were hazy and the fear that perhaps they were not his friends grew in him. Where had all his friends gone? Who were they? He should write to those who would most likely remember him. None of them lived in New York. What was he going there for? To ride the ferry he had never taken all the years he was there? Crane his neck, as he always did, to see the topmost floor of the skyscrapers? The dome of the Empire State Building? What for?

He decided he would not spend the night in a motel. He would park in one of the many rest areas along the way. Anyhow, he was not sleepy. The car radio was on, the outside world was talking to him, singing all those songs that assaulted his mind and eardrums like electronic shocks. He turned it low, and dialed other stations. If he was lucky, he would find one where the songs were old and sweet and sad like blue moon or help me make it through the night. He watched the cars whiz by taking the miles in a whisper of joy. From an old habit back in his early years in America when he didn't own a car, he tried telling what model and make each of the cars that passed him by was. Now he remembered, in those early times, he played a game inventing friends. Perhaps most of the friends he thought he had in New York had only been an invention. What then was not an invention? In his present state of mind, he was not sure. He did not care.

It was nearly morning and his body ached all over. It was the sound of his own moaning that had awakened him. He had fallen asleep behind the wheel. There were meaningless, grating sounds from the static coming from the radio. He turned it off. Only one other car, a station wagon, was anywhere close, parked in the rest area. He was going to turn back to Chicago. It was no problem. A different route, but the scenes looked the same, familiar, drab, and cold.

A jingle from the slums of Manila and the Walled City of Intramuros:

> *Ta ra ra jin pot pot*
> *Americanong supot*
> *Umakyat sa bakod*
> *Na ipit ang itlog.*

Roughly translated:

> *Ta ra ran ta ra ran*
> *Uncircumcised American*
> *Jumped over the bamboo fence*
> *And had his eggs squeezed in between.*

J.P. answered Sol's letter without delay. Without glancing at
the return address, somehow he knew who had written it. Who
else? What feminine hand, those wavy lines, the curlicues, the
gruesome green ink, who else, indeed, but the romantic Sol King,
frustrated actor and half-baked poet, last heard from chanting the
ballads of the stockyards of Chicago. Yes, he was still there.
Strange, but last night, J.P. was thinking of him in connection
with nothing in particular. After all these years. He had expected
something like news about Sol's passing or a letter like this, from
him. Such things happened.

Not too many among those whom J.P. knew during the
thirties in America were still around. He met some in the Philippines the last time he was there, an unhappy breed who never
quite adjusted and complained a lot, wondering aloud what made
them go back when everything—almost—was just fine and dandy in
the United States. Their motives varied: homesickness, fear of
dying alone and being neglected in a faraway land, patriotism,
business, a more respectable and easier way of life. Others had no
motive at all or, having one, never bothered to determine what it
was. These were in the minority. Many more stayed on. They were

all over America. Perhaps right in San Francisco, in those dumps and condemned buildings on Kearny and Stockton, all over California, in dilapidated farm houses and shanties in orange plantations and asparagus fields. But he had lost touch. Many could be dead now.

No, he wouldn't have been surprised at all if he had heard that Sol was dead. And he had completely forgotten him. Now the son of a gun was alive and thinking of visiting him. Was that really what he wrote? The letter was vague. That guy's language was something. He had missed his calling. He should have been a professor. He wowed the ladies with his silver tongue. Of course, he was young then, as all of them were, and quite good looking in an almost effeminate way. He must be an old man now. J.P. wondered how the years had dealt with him.

He wrote: Welcome. Glad you're thinking of visiting San Francisco. About time you did. After all, this is where some of your friends are, I mean, the one or two left, breathing the polluted air of America. Remember Alipio? Pay him a visit, too. See what a second marriage has done to an old man. Almost a cripple, he believes his wife may yet give him a baby. She hasn't had her menopause yet, he claims. He's still good, he says, or, as he puts it, *puede pa.* We'll see about that. Will you believe it if I tell you, he met her the same way he met his first wife? After all, these are rare times as we keep being told. Marriages are no longer made solely in heaven, but quite a few of them, just outside the U.S. Immigration Office.

Your letter was forwarded to me at my new address. You ask about Flora. She's well, I guess. You see, we were separated some time ago. Our divorce became final last year. Now I live by myself. Here in the warehouse where I work. I'll show you around when you come. It's very peaceful here.

The last year before our separation must have been terrible for Flora. She was practically an invalid. Feared she'd lose her job. She had fevers, gradually lost weight and her doctors didn't know why. Until some of her friends advised her to see a psychiatrist who told her after a few sessions that I was the cause, if she didn't get rid of me, she'd be a nervous wreck or worse, go crazy. *Loca.* Well, she believed her psychiatrist. She told me she didn't want to live with me anymore. After 25 years. On our silver wedding anniversary. Almost. The same month, anyway.

Do come and welcome as I say. I'll tell you more. It seems you're retired now or soon will be. No better place than San Francisco to spend the rest of your days. I recommend it. Me.

110

I'm practically retired, too. You'll see. But gee, how time flies, indeed. Don't tell me you're still slaying the ladies with your poetic talks. Take care now and watch your step. Tell me when you're coming. I could meet you. There's nothing much to do here anyhow. Regards. Sincerely, J.P.

J.P. read the letter, his lips moving, breaking in a near smile, his dark brown eyes still young, pensive and shining, in spite of his years. In his light gray robe, the warehouse man's uniform, he looked like an attendant deputy in the house for the aged.

The warehouse was in the basement, one flight below the street level with glass windows so old and dirty, they barely gave the light they were supposed to add to bulbs dangling at every corner between rows of pipes that crisscrossed a ceiling of reinforced concrete. The floor of the warehouse was concrete also. From where he worked, examining and arranging the files, he could see the feet of passersby, mostly workers pushing carts loaded with bolts of paper, showing faintly through the almost opaque glass, although at times, he heard more than saw them. The floor space measured something like the equivalent of the swimming pool he used to own, including the area around it with the spreading multi-colored umbrellas shading lawn tables and chairs, the bathhouses and the mini-golf course enclosed in adobe walls. Maybe bigger. But this was cold cement, not soft carpet grass. Moreover, that was in the past. This was the present. Even so, no regrets.

Perhaps he should have written a longer letter. He should have asked about him, how he was, had he never married, was he travelling alone? He sounded as if he was. There was much to tell, too, but Sol was coming, time enough then, but the poetical guy was vague about it and didn't say when.

J.P. stood up after sealing the envelope and addressing it. He made sure everything was right, postage and all, then threw it into an empty OUT tray on the table. Behind him was a low screened window with glasses pushed open a little to let in some air. It overlooked a concrete segment of the Bay Bridge that came so close to the upper story as it twisted away into the distant mist, that the building seemed like a part of the bridgeway. At this time of the morning, traffic was heavy, but with the wind blowing in the opposite direction, into the sea, the dust was no problem. At night, when he felt cramped and unable to breathe freely in his "cell," he would stand by the window where now he stood and watch the traffic roll by, while below, the boats hardly moved on the water bright with moonlight. The lights from the barges, the oil tanks, and the freighters dotted the river like the lights from the fishing boats back home. In deep winter when the heat in his little makeshift room became oppressive, he would stand here in the dark in his pajamas or undershirt and watch the cargo ships go by. The traffic overhead was a mere distraction of rolling shadows and searching lights. It was the scene below on the river that held him. Mostly he thought of sailing them, no matter where they went, each a bright hint of distant lands. After a while, he just stood there, taking in deep breathing exercises and thinking of nothing at all.

Now, too, he no longer tried to convince himself that this was the best place to be.

That evening he arrived home from work and found all his things packed, he was more surprised that all his personal belongings could be placed in two suitcases and one small valise than in what the packed luggage meant. He had known all along that he had to leave, but he didn't know it was going to be that night. Flora started dialing the phone when he came in, looking a little tired herself and obviously quite unwell as she had been for some time.

"I'm sending for a taxi," she said. "Where do you want to go?"

"May I stay overnight? I'll leave tomorrow, early."

"Where do you want to go? Now."

"You could have called me at the warehouse."

"Where are you going?" Flora asked impatiently while she cupped her hand on the speaker.

"To the warehouse," J.P. said without thinking. There was no other place to go. He didn't have enough money to pay for an overnight stay in a hotel.

As he listened to Flora giving the address, he wondered idly whether, really, all he had was in those suitcases.

"The taxi will be here in a few minutes. If you have some things I haven't put into those suitcases, tell me, I'll have them sent to you. As far as I know, everything's in there."

One of the suitcases was heavy. Flora helped him and as they went down the stairs, lugging the suitcase between them, their fingers touched. She was warm, feverish. Or maybe because he himself had a cold sweat.

When the luggage was safely in the trunk, he opened the cab door to get in, and paused to look back to say goodbye, but Flora had already gone upstairs. All he saw was the light in the hall. It hurt his eyes.

J.P. worked for the Consolidated Insurance Companies, a complex of a dozen insurance firms with offices all over the United States. The main office was in the financial district of San Francisco, within walking distance from the warehouse in which was kept on file all the records of transactions of the twelve companies. J.P. had two assistants, both young men, one black and the other white. Every working day, the mail arrived in pushcarts. All day they sorted it and filed away what had to be added to the records and sent off copies of such documents as were requested by the mother company. J.P. supervised all these. Sometimes he requested extra help when the volume of work warranted it.

Except for a small space which he and his help occupied with their desks and chairs, the entire floor of the warehouse was lined with rows of steel shelves full of filing boxes.

His sleeping quarters consisted of a long flat board covered with brown paper and an army blanket for his bed. In winter when it got too cold, he slept in a sleeping bag which he placed on the flat board. Half-empty steel shelves served as partitions. A cylindrical post, one of several all over the floor that supported the ceiling, formed a side door. He took his meals on a typewriter table on rollers. A pot of coffee stood on an electric burner. A lighted bulb, which he never turned off, hung down a cord from a bar of perforated steel slung diagonally with each end taped around the edge of the shelves on opposite sides. On the shelves, within his reach as he sat on the board, were bottles of instant coffee, aspirin, coffeemate, listerine, boxes of tea bags, granulated sugar, empty porcelain cups, and a roll of toilet paper. A paper cup tied with a string on a middle shelf served as trash bag. Over it, hanging by a wire, was a round face mirror. The other shelves that rounded out this enclosure and made it more private were littered with more empty filing boxes marked Consolidated Insurance Companies, an old San Francisco telephone directory, dirty loafers on the bottom-most shelf, a stray silver spoon among a clutch of plastic ones, cardboards, and a notice pasted on a side wall, which read: "Please help keep our KITCHEN neat & clean," in J.P.'s handwriting.

Nothing fancy. All makeshift. But all for free, utilities and all. In winter, the cement floor was a working refrigerator. What more could he wish? When he went to the manager downtown to ask for permission to utilize a small section of the warehouse as his living quarters, he gave as reason his desire to be alone while writing and collating stuff about his country. After a bit of hesitation and an investigation of the premises, the manager gave him his

113

permission. He didn't ask questions about J.P.'s wife. Surely, they must have known at the main office from his records that he was married. That was one thing he liked about Americans. They minded their own business. In the Philippines . . . why, it seemed, manufacturing rumors was a major industry.

No exaggeration, rumor was a live and fatal aspect of life in the Philippines. He had not been aware of this until after he decided to take Flora there to meet his family. Flora Herd was a native Californian, sunshine and oranges, that sort of thing, bubbly and naive and beautiful. Even now, he could not find it in his heart to blame her completely. For twenty-five years, she stuck to him with a loyalty that should have earned her a row of medals if life were run the way the armed forces were. The comparison was not far-fetched either. Life with Flora Herd, more so during their stay in the Philippines, was war and peace. All the time.

J.P. could without much effort have become like any of his brothers in the Philippines, rich and thriving, and, in their own way, contented and happy. Why not? But life with a tyrannical father and an anemic mother, who suffocated him with her so-called love, made the young Jaime Pardo a rebel and a continual cause of heartbreak for mother and a burden for the chief of the tribe. So at an age when most young men like him in the Philippines were beginning to find fascination in girls and basketball or gambling, J.P. left for the States, completely made up in his mind never to return to the Philippines.

Shortly after the second world war, however, with both parents dead and he, the eldest among the brothers, it was imperative that he be present during the disposition of the considerable property that both his parents had left to their children.

J.P. hesitated. He had a good job in a San Francisco savings and loans institution. He and his wife were popular and respected in the American and Filipino community on the West Coast. He had sworn never to return. Whatever was coming to him as his share of the inheritance he would welcome. He would not question any of the decisions his brothers made. Besides, what would he do with the hundreds of hectares of hemp and coconut lands coming to him, no doubt, unless he lived there himself, or sold them. His first impulse was to write his brothers about his decision.

But the family lawyer flew to San Francisco to talk to him and impressed him with the need for his return. The property was more extensive and valuable than he realized and his brothers, according to the lawyer, had not shown, up to then, the old man's sagacity and genius. And tyranny, J.P. wanted to add.

It was Flora who finally made him change his mind. She wanted to go to the Philippines. She knew then what a wealthy man her husband was in his country, so why not? All this talk about tyranny and vows was pure, unadulterated baloney. Moreover, every American woman she knew who had stayed in the Philippines for any length of time, always had glowing things to say, like maid service, the very low cost of other services and goods, the fantastic social life in Manila. She would make sure they lived in the city or in the suburbs.

Flora deserved an easier life. She had worked hard, taking odd jobs to keep busy and to help out. An extra income came in handy with unexpected expenses becoming more frequent from year to year. They had no children and wanted one, at least. A change of environment, climate and place, might prove beneficial. There was nothing wrong with the couple. J.P. knew that for sure without the doctor's saying so.

How time flew out there in the islands. And what changes it wrought on the unwary, the willing. In no time, Flora had become an altogether different woman. She took the adulation, the crowding of others into her life with grace, with patience, the high color on her cheeks matching the glitter in her blue eyes. She had never been happier. Nor more miserable. A dream and a nightmare. Too good to last. Too bad it lasted that long.

J.P. handled the family interests as everyone hoped he would. In some respects, better. For all his bitterness and love-hate for his father, he soon appeared in the eyes of his brothers and those who worked in the family enterprises, like the old man in his prime. With increasing responsibility, he became more and deeply involved in the social, business, and political maelstrom. Now he seldom saw Flora. She didn't apparently mind this, busy as she was on her own, and enjoying too much a new freedom, a heady vintage of ease, with maids and servants constantly at her service, beauticians vying for her good word, as valuable as a doublespread advertisement in rotogravure of their trade and calling, chauffeurs in monkey suits to drive her to wherever she was going, usually without her husband, who was always somewhere else where she was not.

Before long, she no longer complained about the heat—between walking from their air-conditioned mansion to the air-conditioned car in crowded downtown Escolta, where all the men, including the elderly, stared at her tanned skin, glowing, seductive, in her summer dress. Out on the swimming pool at their own home and in their friends', all the menfolk, most of whom were married, ogled at her as she lay in the sun on the grass in her bikini. In the swimming pool, what she thought at first were accidental brushes from hands and arms on her breasts and thighs were getting too frequent and too accurate to be purely accidental. When she complained about this to J.P., he dismissed the whole idea with a laugh.

"They don't mean a thing," he told her.

"But even the old ones. I don't mind the young men too much . . ."

"Oh, so? But what could the old do? Besides, they don't really mean anything. My countrymen are great admirers of the beautiful."

"I wish they didn't make it too obvious. They scare me. There's that old judge friend of yours. He's so old he can hardly move . . . "

"Ah, good old Judge de Jesus, he's older than my father. Him! You got to beware of him. He's fatal. He tells everybody he has a secret formula from the wild tribes of Makiling."

They laughed together. Those were moments he wanted most to remember. Their laughing together. His pride when she remarked, "Why, everybody in this country speaks English, good English, the maids, the servants, everybody, including their small children. Are you sure you're not Americans in disguise?"

Those moments, indeed. Not the other times. Bad. Ugly. They usually preceded the good times, priceless moments. Like the day she knew for certain that she was going to have a baby because the doctor said so. Thank God, a miracle, J.P. said, adding lightly, "Now, for about nine months at least, nobody, not even that ancient sex maniac with an aphrodisiac, will ogle you." Again, laughter. Strange, faraway sounds now from a distant country, a different world, another time.

In the most natural course of from day-to-day events, J.P. found himself in a high living crowd of the young, rich tycoons, men of influence and power. What was there to resist being drawn in; besides, he could afford it, he felt he belonged; then again, he needed the men in that elite circle to advance his business schemes while he contributed to theirs. A profitable give and take. The time was ripe. The country was recovering from the ruins of war. Money was all important and he had it. It could buy anything. Just anything. Not to mention the fringe benefits. Extra bonuses in illicit pleasures. On their heels, the guilt. The evasions.

116

Sweet, flower-like Flora, there was no end to her amazements, and later, her grief. She believed that the fact that she was going to have a baby was her private affair, shared only with her husband and a few intimate friends. Before long, wherever she went, mere acquaintances, often in the presence of strangers, remarked on her growing abdomen. The first time someone touched it, saying, "Boy or girl?" she slapped her hand away so hard, Flora had to apologize. As far as the other woman was concerned, she didn't have to, as a show of temper was natural in women expecting a baby. By the way, they asked, with you conceiving, what do you do with your husband away most of the time? This is the period of extreme sexuality in a woman, why don't you keep your husband to your side? Of course, how could you, even if you wanted to? Don't you know? Haven't you heard? Poor Flora, of course, you'd be the last one to hear.

The rumor machine was grinding away, slowly at first, but gradually taking on more speed, until full blast, Flora went berserk, nagged her husband, clawed at his face, screamed obscenities, the rare times he was around.

J.P. began to gamble. High stakes. Sometimes with the President of the Philippines and his cabinet men. He was a member of the President's poker cabinet without portfolio but with a sizeable bankroll. This was no rumor, no invention. Now and then, there was exaggeration to excite the fancy about the stakes involved, but that hurt no one more than losers could be hurt by what they did not actually lose. J.P. was a loser. He would never make it in that coterie except in the role of goat, victim par excellence. A lousy bluffer, his face was like an open hand. Strange, but in spite of his losses, his brothers never said a word. Of course, they were making money themselves because of his connections. It was not until much later, back to a life of poverty in the States, that he knew how much of what he was forced to sell to cover losses in the President's Palace, was purchased by his own brothers. At least, his losses in cash were his losses alone. He was solely responsible, and in his own peculiar way of thinking, he was hurting no one but himself. And Flora. That, he knew later and much too late.

For there were other losses, more grievous, which he was soon to know, which he half-expected, but certainly not as cruel as the turn their fortunes had taken. Flora had lost her interest in and her respect for the crowd she went with. There came a time when she was never certain who was her true friend, who her enemy. Everybody had something ill to say, something that hurt without seeming to, usually preceded by a now common, and to her, familiar ploy, a most hypocritical remark, "I won't be telling you this, but I consider you my best friend, practically a sister (or a daughter if the gossip was an elderly matron as was often the case) and for your own good, too, but do you know, I heard . . ."

So the few times J.P. was home, all she did was recite a long litany of names, all strange names to her, names without a body and a face, with whom he was said to be having an affair. True, he had what he considered mild, harmless, tepid flirtations with some of the more aggressive young debutantes who gamboled around the periphery of his circle waiting for trouble—aspiring actresses, secretaries, stewardesses, the hybrid daughters of impoverished Spaniards. "Why, Flor, the world is full of them. It's also full of men waiting for their chance to make them. I happen only to be around. I assure you, as God is my witness, I've never had any affair, really an affair, with anyone."

It turned out, the as-God-is-my-witness vow was the least convincing. It was a bit too much for her, an over-reacting. If anything, it proved he was guilty as hell.

The mills of the rumor industry worked overtime. In J.P.'s household, the war raged on in which each opposing force hurled its most destructive weapon against itself. Beneath the overdone mascara she wore, Flora's illness showed, her secret revealed in her eyes. Now she stayed in her room most of the time. And J.P. had added other vices in which he was reported to indulge.

The day Flora hemorrhaged, she sent for J.P., but he was nowhere to be found. Their servants, his brothers looked for him everywhere he was likely to be, from the Palace to practically all the gambling joints in Manila and the suburbs. Meanwhile, he was up in Baguio, presumably to follow up a deal, but he had been caught up in a mess of good time. He was located in Camp John Hay with some American army officers in a poker game that had already lasted two days and two nights.

When he arrived in the hospital, Flora was asleep. She had had a miscarriage. It was a girl, the doctor said. Flora had lost a lot of blood. She was white as milk. He knew then he had ruined her life. She, more than he, wanted so much to have a child. They should have stayed in San Francisco with the few friends they loved, where there was no crowding, no breaking into the intimacies each shared with the other. What happened? Why?

No sense in asking. Much less in saying, sorry. Sorry for messing your life, Flora, I should have known better, but it was much too late for that now—or was it?

Yet it was not too late then as it was, definitely, now. Something was terribly wrong with him. Make amends?

Flora conceived again and following another quarrel as a direct result of the many rumors she was constantly fed with, she had another miscarriage. This time she nearly died. The deeper she sank into unconsciousness, into what the doctor feared was a subconscious resistance to live, the more J.P. buried himself in vice, which included women, this time, any woman.

Yet both survived. Long after they were back in San Francisco, he could not believe all that had happened to them. In so short a time. But they knew it did. They carried the scars. For him, the payoff in remorse and guilt. But he was almost paid up now. He had always taken care of his dues. Flora had a long memory, but J.P. could not blame her for that. Nor for anything that followed in the wake of the dream turned nightmare in so quick a time. In the backwash, much of the unpleasantness surfaced every now and then, completing the picture of ruin. Before they were aware of it, the years had eliminated them out of the usual opportunities. And J.P., no longer able to remain without a job on the little that still remained for him to take along, soon found himself competing with other naturalized citizens, more experienced men of his age, and younger. It was a downward push and he had lost control. There were days when he spoke not a word, ignoring everything Flora said or did. It was like living with a deaf and dumb person. But he pulled out of that, no thanks to a doctor, but through something he had discovered himself, so he claimed. The only way to peace of mind. When he found a job as warehouse man, he liked it immediately because it gave him the opportunity he needed. For now he wanted all the time to read. No fiction for him, but books on philosophy, religion, the lives of the saints, Zen Buddhism, Christianity. Long before they were separated, J.P. had already separated himself from her—from the rest of the world, he felt—and now dwelt in the realm of books. He was now a student, who had never been much of one; as he once explained to Flora, all the wise men that ever lived were his teachers.

Naturally, he kept getting on her nerves and he was aware of this. What could he do? He was convinced that the truth of life was about to be revealed to him. Now he had the key. The human heart.

In his cell in the warehouse he read past midnight, till dawn on weekends, reading everything there was to read about the human heart. Where had he failed, he used to ask himself. But that was no longer an important nor relevant question. How was he going to live from now on? Keep to his dying day the truth he had discovered or tell it to the world? But how? By writing about it, of course. But he didn't know how to write. His thoughts were beautiful, too much for him to bear in the burden of beauty they laid on his mind, until he started to write them down.

On a lower shelf at the foot of his makeshift bed, there was a box, the right size for the yellow sheets he had been filling it with, on which he had typed his thinking about the truth of the human heart. He felt strange sensations, reading what he had written. That was not the way it sounded in his thoughts, no, not the way it felt in his heart. But it was good writing it down. He could not bear all that in his mind. He would die under the weight of all that truth, some of it so simple it was frightening.

The human heart, that was all that concerned him now even as he supervised the filing of records of persons all over the continent who had mortgaged a bit of their lives against possible death. It was ridiculous. He didn't believe in it at all. But he was lucky he had the job. It was truly meant for him. He believed in miracles. It was nothing short of miraculous that, at his age, under such circumstances, he would have this job, tailored so well to his age and need. It was retirement in action. The only time he would ever retire would be when they found him dead on the long board in the little cubicle he had chosen to spend the rest of his life.

The thought saddened him. Tonight he would talk to the wise ones and, as was his custom now, go down on his knees to pursue his continuing dialogue with God, who had finally shown him the way, the only way. No sadness in that. When J.P. smiled, his uncreased face looked so young. And he was smiling now.

— I'm looking for a Philippine supersitions.
— Pardon? Sorry, the Consulate doesn't handle that data.
— What data?
— Dayta.
— I don't want no dayta. I want superstitions.
— Super . . . superstitions?
— That's it. I'm looking for a Philippine superstitions.
— I see. But perhaps if we talk in Pilipino . . .
— I don't speak no Pilipino. I'm Ilocano.
— That lady in the other room, the Office of the Commercial Attache . . . she speaks Ilocano.
— I'm looking for a Philippine superstitions. Not Ilocano. Why, you don't understand my English? What grade are you?
— Well, never mind. I wish I could help you.
— I wish also.
— Well, here she comes . . . Lyd . . . This gentleman here wants something. Please talk to him. I can't seem to . . .
— Yes?
— Yes. You help me.
— Come with me, please. Sit down.
— I don't want sit down. I want Philippine superstitions.
— Oh. What you want is something on superstitions in the Philippines, a book, a pamphlet.
— Anything. But Philippines.
— Sorry, but we don't have any . . . I mean . . . I'm not aware of any material along that line. Have you consulted the librarian?
— I just come. I have not consulted yet.
— Perhaps she could help you. She's that lady over there. See that small woman trying to reach the topshelf?
— The book of superstitions is in there?
— Ask her. This way, please.
— Yes?
— May I have a book of Philippine superstitions?
— Sorry, we don't carry a book in that category.
— Category? Where can I find them?
— What do you want it for? Perhaps if we sit down together, I can help you out.
— How's that?
— I can make you a list. Of superstitions. Surely, you remember some.
— I don't. That's why I wanna buy.

— But, of course, you must remember some. Like the unlucky Friday the 13th. Seven years' bad luck if you break a glass, bad luck to walk under a ladder . . . Bad luck . . .

— Bad luck. All badluck. What you say is American superstitions. And they ain't true. None of 'em.

- — But these are also our superstitions. They're universal. There are no superstitions I know that are purely Filipino.

— So you don't remember also.

— Of course, I do. What I'm trying to say is that superstitions are what you might call a universal phenomena.

— What's that?

— Phenomena.

— Like dayta?

— That's different. By the way, what do you want Philippine superstitions for?

— For my friend, the Duke. He says we got no Philippine superstitions, we just copycats from the U.S. So I says, he's wrong. We got Philippine superstitions. Exclusive. Genuine. Tell me one, he says. And I says okay. But I can't remember none. I think and think, even sleeping, I think, but nothing, blank.

— Because there's no such thing as an exclusively Philippine superstition.

— There got to be.

— Sorry. None that I know, anyway. Surely, not in this library. Even if there is, it would contain nothing but superstitions and beliefs shared by almost all the people in the world.

— What books you got in there?

— All kinds. Mostly facts and figures on the Philippines. Tourist guides, Philippine periodicals.

— You got Jose Rizal in there?

— I guess so.

— Ha, you're not sure. But no pictures of Rizal. I see the same picture all over this place. Who's he, the owner of the building? You renting from him?

— You must be joking, sir! That's the President of the Philippines.

— Oh, so? Wise guy, I betcha. Maybe he know genuine Philippine superstition.

— Sorry we couldn't be of help.

— I'm sorry also. But I forgive you. Bye!

Not until she wrote it down, bending low over the calendar page on the table, printing each letter as big as JANUARY, did he know what she had been saying every time she named the city where she was going.

"Dowagiac?" Sol said, pronouncing it as well as he could, slowly and carefully, unintentionally stressing the strangeness of the sound.

"Right!" she said in singsong, turning quickly towards the davenport in the living room, alarm in her green eyes, afraid her baby would not be there. Bundled in an army blanket, the child lay on his side sound asleep, a small fist against his sparse blonde hair.

"He's okay," Sol said, watching her eyes soften, erasing years from her face. "And your name is Blanche. With an 'e'—Blanche Hardman. Hard as in not-soft. Man like me. Right?"

"Right!" She gave the word a lilt that made it sound like the opening phrase of a refrain cheer leaders chant. "You talk like the man in the employment office, 'cept you're funnier."

She was sitting at the table in the kitchen, sipping her coffee, her hands around the cup.

"Lord, it's warm in here," were her first words as soon as they came in, the baby wrapped up and tucked inside the coat she was wearing. The blizzard was still raging outside. He had driven cautiously in the swirling snowstorm through slushy streets.

"I told you," Sol had answered. "And you got nothing to worry about." He had to keep reassuring her. She was obviously uneasy and perhaps quite nervous.

His decision to go inside the Greyhound Bus Depot on Clark and Randolph was an impulse. He had no business being out on such a day with the wind hissing through the electric wires in a fury to snap them all, venting its frustration on loosely hung shingles and signs that crashed and rolled on the pavements with a deafening clatter. Cut wire, charged and dripping low, and those sharp-edged boards mostly made of tin, could kill. The streets were nearly deserted. Only a few traffic officers, in raincoats and galoshes, were out, shooing occasional pedestrians into the nearest subway entrances, shouting to them to get out of the streets, blowing their whistles, like cries for help on a day turned into night. He had missed the weather report that afternoon. He was already downtown before he realized what a day it was going to be. Too far and too risky to drive back to Honore Street. He had to park somewhere. Cruising along Randolph past the Chicago Civic Center, he saw a spot where a car was pulling out, and without losing time, he maneuvered expertly into the vacated space. Even then, he was still undecided on what to do, but as he peered through the blurring windshield, he noticed he was close to the bus depot, right at the main door. He had thought of visiting the place for information in case he decided to do some of his travelling by bus.

His so-called long vacation had not yet started. Something was always turning up that was causing some delay. Important things, he called them, but they were actually trivial, not at all necessary nor really important enough to require his time and attention. The truth was, he did not want to leave the apartment. Up to then, he had not told his landlord about his travel plans. In fact, he didn't know what his plans were except that he was certain he was going away. Where, he didn't know. That was why those old pictures were still scattered all over the apartment. He had to push some of them off the davenport to give place for the baby. He meant to go over them again, to try as best as he could to refresh his memory. He might find one or two to whom he could write and visit. Yet he could not recall most of the faces. Strange, but his mind seemed to have taken a peculiar turn. He could now recall without difficulty friends of his youth in the faraway country—not only their names and faces but incidents shared with them, including the occasions when the pictures were taken. It was the years close to the present that were farthest away. His mind was made up on one thing: if the end didn't come while he was traveling, he was going back to his apartment and stay until he died, which should be soon enough. He knew. In his absence, therefore, he intended to continue making monthly rental payments. Indeed, the more he thought about it—the vagueness of his travel plans in particular—there was no telling that he might be able to come back. He was absolutely certain, however, that the end was near, but how near and when, this he did not know and did not wish to know.

These past months while he busied himself with what he considered necessary preparation for what was not only imminent but inevitable, there were times when he actually felt well, spent days and nights in succession without the usual pains. Recently, with cold weather settling in early long before Christmas, every part of his body was marked for pain. A creeping ache that jabbed at its first approach sent answering shivers of pain all over his body. He writhed and groaned, opening frantically whatever bottle was close at hand. All of them were pain-killers anyhow, prescribed "as many times as needed," with any number of refills allowed. There had been moments when the pain ceased dramatically seconds after he had swallowed the pills, but he noted that whatever respite from pain he got from these action-in-seconds drugs, he had to pay in long lingering greater pain afterwards. These body pains had tormented him for the last two or three years. It seemed like a lifetime and he had somehow learned to bear them while they lasted. The doctors had diagnosed his ailment as arthritis, something, they consoled him, that came with age. Everyone suffered from it in one form or another after middle age. Lately, he was convinced that his pains were due to something worse than the doctors surmised. His blood pressure, his heart murmurs, the dizzy spells, were variants and symptoms of what truly ailed him, whatever medical name they called it.

Perhaps retirement was not such a good idea. When busy in his work, the pains occurred only at bedtime. Now that he had nothing to do, he could feel the pains practically all the time.

So he kept busy. All the months after that day in June when he knew that the time had come for him to retire and begin traveling, he always had something "important" to do in preparation for his extensive trip. He was going to travel all over the

United States, visit the cities where he had lived before. With some luck, he might yet see such old friends as had been close and dear. Often, alone in his apartment, he called out the names he remembered, willing them to think of him also as he was thinking of them. It was not easy deciding, in the last few years, to live a life alone without companionship, involvements, love affairs, but the price in heart-break was too much. Those he had loved dearest had hurt him most. Whom had he hurt most? Comparing wounds was a miserable pastime. The way he had chosen was the best. No more involvements now, no more depending on others, no more intimacies. Better the strangers. They were often the kindest givers, the most grateful for the meanest present.

If there was time, he could go abroad. Perhaps return to the Philippines. He shook his head at the idea. That would be the worst yet, coming back the way he was to those scenes over which, he loved to say, the final curtains had fallen.

Other places in the world were waiting. He could go to them. Yes. By now he had visited practically every airline agency and travel office along Michigan Avenue and similar places downtown, asking questions, collecting travel posters, and, whenever he could, bringing home huge color posters of various countries in the world.

He took time all through the autumn months to spread them out in his apartment, pasting them on every available space on the walls with masking tape. He had chosen from his collection only those he liked for one reason or another or for no reason at all except that he thought the pictures were pretty or extremely big. Enlarged, blown-up pictures had always fascinated him. The walls in his apartment had remained bare because he didn't want to hang anything small on them. The bareness of the walls did not bother him. He was used to it. Now pictures were everywhere, on the walls in the kitchen, the bathroom, and, of course, the living room. He had a special picture for his bedroom, the ruins of the Acropolis, which he had pasted on the wall at the foot of his bed, framing it neatly with masking tape. Gazing at it, he felt the dust of powdered stones touch his face, and always, it reminded him of war pictures showing direct bomb hits. Those on the other walls, including the panel on the inside of the door that separated the living room from the bedroom, were placid, comfortable scenes largely done in green, his favorite color: the Alpine mountains in Switzerland, the Arc de Triomphe on the Champ de Elysees, the Taj Mahal, its shadows pure black in the moonlight, and a Philippine maiden wearing a *buri* hat, ripe and luscious in a lacy blouse and many-colored skirt against a background of Mount Mayon shaped like a ponderous breast.

A huge poster lay on an old throw rug in the living room, of a Javanese dancer with nails longer than her fingers, pendant earrings that reached to her brown shoulders, a heart-shaped face beneath a glittering tiara. Some of the snapshots and photographs lay on top of it, seeming to blind an eye, cutting off some of the dancer's fingernails, hiding the sequins on her breasts.

"Lord, what have you here, a picture show?" Blanche had asked, looking dazedly about her in the kitchen.

"Wait till you see the others," Sol said.

"This one on the floor, you got no more place for it, huh?"

"Yep."

"These old pictures, shall I . . . ?"

"No, please. Just leave 'em there."

"Sorry . . . say, have you been to all these places?"

"No. I mean not yet."

"You're going, huh?"

Blanche appeared to be slowly getting used to the apartment and, of course, the situation.

🦋

𝒱

The bus depot was full of people. All the seats in the waiting areas were occupied, sometimes with duffle bags, suitcases, trunks, back-packs. Along the walls, clear way around, groups of bedraggled looking young people were sitting on the floor, asleep or trying to sleep.

Later he learned that the blizzard was general in the midwest. All the regular bus schedules had been cancelled. The circular counter in the center of the main floor was crowded with travelers seeking information. The employees on duty, two men and one woman, appeared about ready to drop, their lips barely moving, their eyes half closed, their fingers tracing numbers on the printed schedules like automatic pointers on a medical chart. Above the din of voices, shuffle of feet, clatter from the game room, the static from the loudspeakers, rose the announcer's voice calling attention to bus arrivals but not a word on scheduled departures. Wait for further announcements. Wait. Please wait. And thank you for traveling Greyhound!

Courtesy in crisis, Sol thought, quite unaffected by it. What a time he had chosen for seeking information on bus schedules. Yet Sol didn't mind being there. It was a warm, comfortable place.

With his coat on, he felt good. Unbuttoning it, he felt even better, more relaxed, part of a mass, for the present safe and dry. There was no way of knowing who were passengers or who were not, who were simply getting out of the wicked weather outside. Some passengers carried no luggage. Others carried the whole world, it seemed, with all that luggage surrounding them like sandbags against rising waters. Piles of newspapers and empty paper and plastic bags lay at the foot of seats among cigarette butts and empty packs. A cleaning man was picking them up as he went about, sweeping the floor with an enormous mop. Uniformed policemen, security guards, mostly black and brown, stood by glancing around, answering questions, laughing among themselves. A few oriental-looking men and women raised their heads from the papers they were reading as he passed in front of them and, as quickly, returned to their reading. Chinese, most of them, no doubt, Sol thought. Another Filipino like him would smile. Or would he?

The girl wore a man's shirt a bit too large for her. Her denim pants were tight and reached up above her ankles showing bare feet in discolored canvas shoes. What struck Sol was not the shabbiness, the rumpled hair and the dirt-stained shirt, but the look in her eyes, like a wounded bird's as she cuddled a baby in her arms. The child's legs stuck out and all it had was a frayed sweater. The girl—no more than a child herself although her face was an adult's, and her arms were blotchy—held the baby tightly to her breast, touching its feet now and then, obviously to keep them warm. Mother and child were cold. Even in the warm waiting room full of people, they were cold. Perhaps hungry. There was a paper bag filled with baby things, no doubt, at her feet on the floor. It seemed she had no other luggage.

Unaware of what he was doing, Sol stared at the girl. He passed her once, walked back, then stood in front of her and stared at her again. When he realized it, he looked around to see whether any-one had noticed him. Nobody. Everyone else was minding his own business, mostly waiting for further developments, ears perked for announcements about changes in the weather and schedules.

The young mother herself did not seem to notice him. Now he stood close enough for her not to be aware of his presence. He had no recollection of exactly what he said to open up a conversation. All he remembered later was that the girl, without shyness or evasion, was telling him that she had come from Joliet; she was on her way to Dowagiac. She had not expected the delay. When her bus arrived in Chicago, it was not snowing hard. If there was no bus passing through Dowagiac that night, she would have to wait in the bus depot until regular trips were resumed and no one seemed to know when for sure. When he remarked that the child must be cold, she pressed it closer to her breast, covering the child's feet alternately with her hand.

"You're cold yourself. May I help?" Sol said, not thinking too much of what he was saying or its possible implication. It was not like him till now to speak to strangers with such earnest concern. Certainly not to women. That part of his life with all its memories was well behind him. It was not easy for the sort of person that he was—caring, compassionate—but he had made it. Sheer will power. And Fate, which he believed in, surely must have helped. His choice was the course his life was bound to take—no more involvements. Now this. What had come over him? He should have kept away. He shouldn't have asked.

Clasping the sweater around the child's body, the girl said nothing. Sol noticed it was not a sweater but a sleeveless shirt, maybe the mother's, and awfully inadequate.

"Look," Sol said, "I'll be back."

He remembered the extra coat in his car, on which he used to sit or wrap around his legs when the heater was slow in starting. He waited a while for a lull in the storm before rushing out to his car to get the coat. A gust lashed at him, driving him inside. Aw heck, he said, peering through the glass doors, and waited for another chance. This time he made it, clutching the coat as he went back. It was terrible outside. Perhaps he wouldn't be able to leave the depot himself that night.

He went direct to the Post cafeteria and bought a cup of coffee which he brought to the girl.

"Here," he said, giving her the cup, "this should help. And here's a coat."

The girl stretched one pale reddish arm towards the cup and took a sip. Her lips trembled when she tried to thank him. After another sip, she looked up at him, biting her lips.

"Feel better?" he asked.

The girl nodded as tears rolled down her cheeks. With the hand that held the cup, she tried to brush them away.

"Watch out now, you'll spill the coffee on the little one," he said. She smiled, but the tears continued to fall.

"If you want to go to the restroom, go ahead. I'll watch the baby. And put this on. It may not fit you well, but . . ."

"Thanks," she said, doing as she was told. "He won't wake up," she assured him, "but if he does . . ." She dipped her hand into the paper bag and took time getting out what she wanted. Finally, she held an empty milk bottle, which she hastily put back. "He won't wake up," she said as she walked away.

"You better not wake up," he told the baby, "before mommy comes back." He removed his coat and jacket, then peeled off the cardigan he had on over a vest and placed it gently around the sleeping baby. He put on his jacket and the overcoat and waited. He peeped into the paper bag and saw pieces of clothing that must have been diapers and a rattler. He had made up his mind to invite her to eat at the cafeteria, wait for further announcements and see them off to wherever that funny-sounding town she was going to. However, the way it looked outside, she might have to stay and wait until morning.

The coat looked a bit too big for her, but nobody would notice that as most boys and girls were wearing all sorts of outlandish garments without regard for what was oversized or ill-fitting. She had washed her face. She looked even paler. Now he noticed that her eyes were green. He wanted to tell her, your eyes are green, but what a thing to say. What was happening to him? He was acting without much thought and likely to say things he ought not to say, if he was not too careful.

"Did he bother you?" she asked, sitting beside the empty seat nearby, which he had been occupying. When she noticed the sweater around the child, she touched it in a gesture of disbelief and gratitude—what else—saying faintly, "Thanks . . ." Sol shook his head.

"Feel better now?" he asked again.

"Thanks, yes," she said, barely moving her lips as she looked at him squarely.

"And now you can eat something," he said, adding hastily, "There's no telling when you can leave, you know. I'll get you a sandwich. What would you like?"

She turned away from him, her eyes searching every other nook and spot in the crowded floor for a way out from whatever it was, the way her head moved ever so slightly. When she looked at him again, the clean face was crinkly, old. "You've been so kind," she said. "I really . . . I don't think I should . . ."

"No bother," he said. Something in his tone, perhaps the look in his face—a smile touched her lips.

"I'd like to . . . Jerry's no more milk," she said. She dipped her hand into the bag and took the empty bottle out. "It's empty. I didn't bring any extra. I thought . . ."

Sol took the bottle from her hand. "Ordinary milk will do?"

he asked.

"Yes," she said.

"Wouldn't it be too cold?" he asked.

"Oh, no. It's okay."

When he returned, he had a clean bottle full of milk. Sure, it was cold, but the baby was still fast asleep. He brought her sandwiches wrapped in cellophane.

"Here," he said, giving her the sandwiches. That's corned beef and tuna there. If you like, I'm going back for coffee."

"It's okay. Don't bother."

She held the sandwiches, glancing at them every now and then, not knowing what to do.

"You're supposed to eat 'em," Sol said.

She began to open one, then paused, saying, "Have one."

"No, thanks. They're yours. Go ahead, eat 'em."

He excused himself as Blanche began to eat because he felt she would feel more at ease if he were not around watching her. He found a place hidden away behind the stairway back of the main entrance. There were more people, coming in from buses that barely made it to Chicago. He was sure there would be no let-up in the weather. The loudspeakers were silent. They had been silent for the past hour, he guessed.

He could not understand himself. What he was doing, what he had done, what he was intending to do. A mild form of recklessness had taken possession of his will, his reason. He didn't care, whatever it was, right or wrong. Enough that at this moment, he felt good, so good, he felt like crying himself. He could move about, on his feet or sitting down without feeling an ache in his joints or a pain stabbing at him between the ribs or at the back of his head.

From where he was sitting, he could see that the baby was awake now. She was feeding him. The milk would just be right, he was thinking. The mother looked so small, his coat nearly hiding her face. She'd be warm. Joliet, that's where she came from. That's right. He knew about Joliet, but he could be wrong. It was none of his business. And she was going some place with a crazy name. Now perhaps he should talk to her again.

The baby was sucking at an empty bottle. "This the kind man I was telling you, Jerry," she spoke to the child. Jerry sucked on and wouldn't let go when the mother tried to take the bottle away. "Be a good boy . . . there . . . there . . ."

"He needs another bottle," Sol suggested.

"That's okey," the girl said. "I left him a sandwich." She had not eaten one of them.

"He might not like it."

"It's okay. Here's something for you, sweetheart," she said, unwrapping the sandwich. Jerry raised his hand to grab it, but she moved it out of his reach.

Sol sat beside them, watching them play out a game mother and child must have done before numberless times. He felt good watching them. He felt well. Here was something he had not known before. Yet he didn't know what it was and he didn't give a damn.

A voice boomed from the loudspeakers. May I have your attention, please, it said. As Sol had expected, the highways were impassable from as far north as Michigan and all of the midwest. No change in the weather condition was expected until tomorrow morning.

"Where's this place you're going?"

She gave him the name again, adding, "That's in Michigan."

"What are you going to do now?"

"Wait. What else?" Then as if the thought had just struck her, she asked, "And you, where you going?"

"Nowhere," he said.

"I thought so. You have a car out there. You're meeting someone."

"No, I'm not. I came to ask for some information."

"You're going some place."

"Yes. But not now."

"If I had a car I'd take no damn bus."

"I'm not sure I would, myself. I was figuring . . ."

"Any time you want to go, I'll give your coat back. And your sweater. I don't know how I can thank you. Say thank you to the kind man, Jerry."

Jerry made sounds and threw him a glance, then got busy with the tuna. The mayonnaise was all over his face, but his mother didn't bother to wipe it off.

"No hurry. I'll wait," Sol said, not knowing why or what for. It didn't occur to him that he might have to wait until morning.

"Oh, no, that's okay," the girl said. "You don't have to. And here's your coat."

Sol touched her shoulder to keep her from standing and taking off the coat.

"I got a better idea," he said, "but I don't know how you'd take it. You see, you could spend the night at my place. You and the baby would be comfortable there. I'm sure you could sleep and rest. It's a warm place."

As he talked, he noticed that the girl was staring at him and she had the same look in her face before the tears came. Sol shook his head, smiling in spite of himself. "I knew it. I'd scare you. But I wish you would understand . . . Well, it was too much to expect. I don't blame you. A perfect stranger . . ."

"I didn't mean . . ." the girl began and paused, a frown on her face. She appeared to be in deep thought over something that was troubling her and she didn't quite know what she was going to say or do. "You've done lots. You're so kind."

"You said that before," he said. "Please don't say that again. It's no big thing, really. Anyone, anyone like me who didn't have a thing to do, would have helped you. The policeman over there, or anybody, would have looked after you."

A dark look came into her face as she said, "Oh, no, I won't have nothing to do with 'em police."

"So forget I asked." The seriousness in his tone was not completely lost on the girl. The cloud in her face had lifted considerably.

"I'd sooner go with you," she said, glancing quickly towards the uniformed men.

"Jerry's not eating anymore. He's just playing with the bread," Sol said.

"Jerry, you stop that," the girl said, taking the mashed bread from him, as she added softly without looking at Sol, "You live far from here?"

"On the south side. I live alone."

"Oh."

"My name's Sol King."

Her face showed puzzlement. He gave his name again.

"I'm Blanche," she said, "Blanche Hardman."

Sol didn't get the name either, that is, he was not sure he did, but it didn't matter. He was worried over his concern for this girl and the child. The seriousness of his invitation. Something he could not understand was urging him to take care of them, to make these few hours more comfortable for both. He was now trying to convince himself that it was fate that sent him to the depot. He had been too engrossed with himself. All these late years. Was that it, really? Had he really been too self-centered, closing his eyes to everything that did not concern him? Or had he been fooling himself? Could it be that it was the girl, not her plight, that attracted him to her? Physically. Her green eyes. Crazy. He had seen other girls prettier. Yes, but not as helpless. Without that look in their eyes like a wounded bird's, remember? Crazy. Why, his first impression of her was one of untidiness, filth, that she would smell if he came near. She must have been wearing that shirt and those denim pants for days or weeks without changing or taking a bath. She was not pretty. The blotches on her arms must be all over her body. There were blemishes on her face. She could be suffering from a contagious disease.

No, it couldn't have been physical. For the past few years, he had not wanted a woman. The thought and the craving for woman flesh had dissipated with the passing years and his increasing dependence on pain killers must have helped. Perhaps drugs killed something else like sex. In the few years in Chicago when he was not yet too old, after finally swearing off any involvement of whatever nature after a succession of unfortunate relations with women that left him embittered and half-crazy, there were times when he missed and longed for the sort of warmth only a woman, a woman in love, could give. He thought he would not be able to live without one. He had been with them too much all his younger life. It was not easy to drop a whole pattern of existence. But he lived through the most critical times of need that drove him to something like self-pity until a numbness set in, a cooling of passion. Even the memory of past delights was not much of a prod to push him on headlong into more relationships in the ensuing years. After a while, he didn't think much anymore of being alone. His work occupied him. And the little games and hobbies he had invented to pass the time: sorting his file of envelopes, classifying their contents—pictures according to background, city and country (Philippines or United States); cancelled checks and receipts from way back (sometimes a purchase let loose a flood of memories as clear as yesterday's good kiss). He enjoyed estimating to the cent how much he had in cash and in savings, how much he would likely have at the end of any given number of years, how much was coming to him in pension and benefits. He passed the time listening to his stereo, the radio, watching television. Even his pains afforded him a chance to pass the time like when the pains were quite bearable, he timed how long they lasted, the intervals between seizures. Occasionally, when he met a happy-looking man with a wife and children, he wondered whether he had made the best choice or had given up too soon like a coward wallowing in self-pity.

"Think about it," he said, feeling that the decision should be purely voluntary on her part. If he had unwittingly shown over-anxiety to make her go with him, he wanted to dispel the impression. "I don't want you to do anything you don't want. I said I'm going to stay and wait, but if you don't want me to, say so. You may keep the coat and the sweater."

"Oh, no, no! You've done too much already."

"I'll be frank with you," Sol said, pursuing his own thoughts; "I won't blame you for not accepting my invitation. Don't feel obliged. I'm a stranger as you are. But look, I'm old, can't you see I'm a very old man?"

"Funny, you should say that," she said, chuckling. "I was just now trying to guess how old you are. Perhaps you're not as old as you sound."

"Do I sound old?"

"A little."

"There you are."

"But I've decided you're not really old."

"Suit yourself. The invitation stands."

She stood up with the child in her arms, wrapped Sol's cardigan around his little body, and placed his legs inside her coat as she stooped to get the paper bag.

"Let me carry this," Sol said.

"Please, no," she said, taking the bag away from him. "It stinks."

Sol who thought he had a dog's sense of smell could not smell anything. Funny.

As they walked up the escalator, she said, "Sure it's okay?"

"That's for you to decide. You're a big girl now."

"Now you sound like dad."

"I could be, too."

On their way out the main exit, he said, like an established member of the family, "Sure you got everything? Your tickets?"

"In my purse, in here," she answered, lifting the paper bag a little.

Fortunately there was a lull in the storm. It was hard to see in the blowing snow.

"Warm enough?" he asked as he drove on carefully. She had edged closer to his side. He felt her quick warmth and her smell. Unpleasant. Bad. His dog sense was working now. Perhaps it was not she. It could be the paper bag he had placed on the floor back of him. He felt like gagging and opening the window on his side a little bit. But she might notice it. The car had been moving at a turtle's pace. He stepped on the gas as he could hardly breathe.

They were almost there. Somewhere, far up among the tall buildings, the wind hissed. The child in her arms was practically

136

inside the coat. How could he breathe inside the enveloping wool, would he not suffocate, Sol wondered, worrying more about the child than the condition of the roads. The smell was still there, overpowering. Perhaps he was driving faster than he should. Suppose . . . oh, God. He feared there might be fallen trees across the streets on the way. If he had to make a detour, he was not sure he would be able to stand it.

"Lord, it's warm in here," she said as soon as the door closed behind them.

Sol busied himself with the air sprays immediately, saying the apartment was stuffy, he had been out the whole day. Blanche held on to the baby. She had placed the bag near the sink, which was closest to the door.

"Get inside. Go on in," Sol said, making circular motions with the air spray. "Put him on the davenport. He'll be comfortable there. Wait . . . excuse me." He cleared the davenport, pushing away everything on it to the floor and spread an army blanket, folded length-wise in two.

"There you go." He began to spray the living room, directing the spray towards the ceiling, away from the davenport. "I'll get him something warm as soon as I'm through with this. Does he like hot soup? I bet he does . . . Hey, smells good, no?"

Blanche sniffed. "Smells like fruit."

"Lemon."

"Sure is."

"The bathroom's in there beyond that door," he said, pointing to the bedroom on the farther side of the living room. "Go in there if you want to."

She removed the coat she was wearing and walked towards the bathroom through the open door to the bedroom.

"Don't forget the bag," he called out to her.

"Sorry," Blanche said, half running towards the kitchen. She picked up the bag and brought it with her to the bathroom.

Sol directed the spray on the spot where the bag had stood, saying to himself, over and over, shame on me, I'm a dog, shame . . .

Jerry lay on his stomach, his head on one side, facing the back of the sofa. Sol peered at his face to be sure; Blanche had wrapped him up so well, the child might not be able to breathe freely. How soundly he slept.

Sol could hear the water running, splashing. She must be washing Jerry's dirty things. Was she also taking a bath? He hoped so.

As he listened, he could not tell. But it was taking her long, whatever she was doing. The clock above the stove showed it was past ten. That late already? The moaning of high winds reached his ears faintly. Now and then, the clatter of tin cans rolling down the street. Perhaps later they would have a late snack. The refrigerator was full. As always. Oranges, apples. A cold plate of apple pie, meats and bottles of water. He hated drinking tap water no matter how cold it was, it was never cold enough for him and there was a taste to it that he didn't like. But water from the bottle kept long in the refrigerator was excellent, almost sweet in its tastelessness, a perfect drink after a meal. He would ask her what she wanted to eat. There were tins of canned foods, soups and meat. There was milk, too, but very little. Enough for tonight, anyhow. On their way back to the depot the next day, he would get Jerry some. Other things besides. Surely by then, the storm would be over, the highways cleared, and all bus schedules back to normal again.

He felt something was amiss. For all his constant prattle and movement, he was not doing well enough. He had forgotten something. Then he knew what it was. He knocked his head lightly with his fist. Where are your brains, Solomon King, he asked himself. He should have thought of it earlier. He rushed to the living room, and, standing at the door of his bedroom, he waited until the splashing and the sound of running water had ceased. Then he called, "Blanche!" She must have heard him because she turned off the faucets abruptly perhaps to make sure. There was complete silence in the bathroom.

"Blanche!" he called again.

"What?" she shouted back.

"Listen. Take your time. There are towels in the cabinet in there. Take a bath if you wish. I'll have some clothes for you to wear when you're through. I'll leave 'em on the bed. You hear?"

"Sure. Okay. Thanks."

Sol found a couple of shirts in his closet which she could wear. And slacks. Clean denim pants he had not worn for years and should be in fashion now. The shirts were good as new, broadcloth, polyester and cotton, drip dry. They would be a bit too large, but they would do meanwhile. Now he was certain she had no change of clothes. She could wash what she had. Even if they didn't dry up, she could take them with her. She could keep what she could wear of his own.

He placed the shirts and slacks on the bed, and the denim pants which he thought she might want to wear. The ceiling light was dim so he turned on the bed lamp so that it would be easier for her to make a choice. As he closed the door behind him to go to the living room, he heard a lot of splashing and running water.

While he waited, he passed the time considering what he called the workings of fate that sent him to the bus depot to help out Blanche and Jerry.

This was no test. Too late for that and definitely uncalled for. More than anything else, the incident was an opportunity for him to do what he ought to do at this late hour. Also, it was a sign, fate's finger pointing in the direction to which his life—these remaining days of his life—was taking him.

Everything was shaping up as he had anticipated.

When she came out of the bedroom, she was wearing the polyester cotton shirt, a shade of green, the color of banana leaves, and the dark brown denim pants. She had rolled up the sleeves and knotted the front of the shirt tight enough to hold up the trousers as they could be a bit loose although they seemed to fit her.

"Sorry, it took me too long," she said.

He gestured to mean it was all right, he didn't mind.

"Your clothes are real nice."

"Thanks. You know, I don't need any of those any more."

"What d'ya mean?"

He shrugged his shoulders.

"What you going to do with 'em?"

"Give 'em away. Choose what you want. Take 'em all."

"I'd need a suitcase."

"I'll give you one."

"Oh, no. I didn't mean that. And I haven't thanked you yet for these," she said, passing her hands over her sides, touching part of the shirt and the pants she was wearing.

Sol went to the kitchen where she joined him later after staying a while with the baby. They sat facing each other at the table and talked, each wondering how it was outside. They could hear the storm blowing. They ate when they felt hungry. Sol was careful not to ask too many questions. There was no need to. She talked as she pleased. Every now and then she went to the living room to see Jerry whom, she said, she had decided to bathe first thing in the morning.

"Call Greyhound for me, please, will you, please, soon as you're up in the morning?"

"Will do," he answered, trying to get into the rhythm of her speech, the way she talked, her inflection and her words, her phrasing. "How about calling Dowagiac right now?"

"Don't have to. Nobody's expecting me."

"Your folks?"

"Mom and her husband. Dad, he died in an accident."

He didn't have to wait on her. She evidently wanted to be useful or she was not used to being served. She heated the soup herself. No, she didn't want anything else. "I'd get sick if I took another bite," she said.

Sol was curious to know more about her, but he refrained from appearing too nosey. She talked, however, quite freely.

She explained that she stayed with her married mother in Dowagiac who babysat while Blanche worked in a factory that manufactured hooks, all sizes, some of 'em so big they could be for sharks or less. All she did all day was sorta sorted 'em for size and defects. She useta get her fingers all bloodied, but later it didn't hurt no more. Could be her palms got no more blood in 'em. Was not much fun but it was a living. Enough for expenses which included what she paid mother every week. During her pregnancy she worked up to the very day her baby came, returning to work a couple of weeks later. 'Twas okay. She was strong. Besides, she needed the money. Why, did he think she got free board and lodging?

"No way. Mom got expenses too. Mom and him liked to live it up. Me, I don't drink, I don't smoke. I like going to movies, that's all. That Jerry has been to a lot of 'em, yes, sleeping in my arms most of the time. When I save enough I go to Joliet. That's where Jerry's dad's at. I bring him cigarettes, comic books."

Jerry's dad was younger than her and crazy about comic books, smoked a lot, too. At this point in her story, Sol got the impression she must be older than she looked unless her husband was still in his teens.

"This the first time he seen Jerry. Jerry surprised him he can walk. It was fun watching the two. He don't want us to go yet, but I'd given him all the cash I have because I got a roundtrip, see. We'll be seeing him again real soon. There's a mufflers shop where I can work and save more."

"How much longer will he be in Joliet?"

"Won't be long now. We write each other."

Later that night, she told him, "Looks like you got problems too."

"Not really," he said. "My only problem is I got no problem."

"You're funny. You remind me of a Mex I knew. You're not Mex. I thought not. But you talk like one. You look like one I could've sworn."

"I don't look like nobody," he said, a weariness in his tone.

140

The implication of what he had just said was not lost on him.

"Bet you wanna rest now. Go ahead. I'll sleep with Jerry. I always do."

"You two can stay in my room," he said. "I'll be comfortable in the living room."

"No, no. Thanks, Go ahead. We'll be okay here."

"Sure?"

"I'm sure."

He brought out blankets and sheets and a pillow. "You can keep the light on if you wish," he said.

"That's okay. Thanks."

"Good night," he said, walking to his bedroom. As an afterthought, he added, "I'll leave the door open in case you or Jerry want to use the bathroom."

"Okay," she said so softly, he was not sure she had spoken.

As he lay down, he heard a switch click. She had turned off the light. The wind had died down. For a long time he lay awake, listening. He heard nothing. He felt nothing. Tonight he didn't have to take a single pill. He turned on his side and was soon sound asleep.

"Did I frighten you?" Sol asked as he closed the door behind him, a bag of groceries in his arms. It was almost noon.

"Nooo . . .," Blanche yawned, sleep still in her eyes. Jerry was playing on the floor in the kitchen. He smiled when he saw Sol come in.

"When I woke up you two were fast asleep. I thought I'd get some groceries. Milk for Jerry. Why is he in the kitchen? It's cold in here."

"I didn't want him to mess up those things on the floor in the other room."

"Beautiful out. Storm's over, streets are clear. Snowdrifts all over the sidewalks."

"How about Greyhound?"

"Schedules back to normal. The earliest for Dowagiac would be this evening. Same trip you missed."

"We better get going."

"No hurry. Let's have something to eat. You must be starved."

"Jerry, he wants his milk. Sol, thanks."

He prepared breakfast, brunch, he called it. Blanche helped when she was not attending to the baby. He was delighted when Jerry walked towards him with the empty milk bottle still frothing at the nipple raised in one hand. He scooped up the little one and swung him around with a strength he had not felt before he still had in him. It felt so good he wanted to keep swinging him until Jerry hollered with more glee than fright and she kept saying something he couldn't make out. Finally, he stood him on the floor, saying, "He reminds me of a butcher friend, they walk the same."

Jerry toddled back and forth between Blanche and Sol's outstretched arms. "He's fantastic," he exclaimed, hugging the excited child, who didn't seem to tire walking back and forth, but when he burped in Sol's arms, she snatched him away.

"I don't know what has come over him. I better give him his bath now, he might throw up."

Sol felt they took too long in the bathroom. He was eager to see Jerry, clean and fresh, and hold him in his arms. When the bathroom door opened, he was waiting for them. He took the child from his mother's arms.

"Jerry's things are all dry now, but mine's still wet. I shouldn't have washed 'em."

"That's fine," Sol said, walking to the living room with Jerry. "Keep what you're wearing. And if you wish—you see, I got lotsa clothes I won't be needing anymore. Take all you want."

"Oh, Sol!"

"Wish I had something for Jerry, too. What do you want, Jerry boy?" He had snuggled in his arms, his damp head on Sol's shoulder, his weight just right and pleasurably warm. He was going to buy him anything if he only had the time, but they were leaving. Perhaps they should start early enough so that he could take them to a store that sold baby things.

"You're spoiling him," Blanche was saying.

Sol insisted that she take with her any of the old shirts and slacks he had taken out of the closet and spread on the bed.

"Are you sure you really want me to have all these?" Blanche asked, touching them, pressing them to her bosom. "And what about you?"

"I don't need them. In fact, before I leave for my vacation—I think I've told you about it—I intend to give away most of my clothes. Won't be needing them anymore."

"Aren't you coming back ever?"

"Perhaps. But even if I did, I won't need all I got."

"You sound funny, Sol. Like you know something's gonna happen, like you're gonna disappear."

He tried to explain, how he planned to visit places, particularly where he had once lived to visit with old friends whom he had not seen or heard from in twenty, thirty years, maybe longer. A lifetime really. He was retired. There was nothing much left for him to do. And he definitely didn't intend to keep all his belongings in storage. Clothes are for people to wear. Lotsa people don't have enough to keep 'em warm.

Blanche listened attentively while she went over the clothes spread out before her with no apparent interest. She wanted to take the baby from him and at first he said no. Soon, however, he felt a bit tired so he put him down and they played a little. Blanche glanced towards them once in a while as she sat on the bed apparently trying to make up her mind what to choose. She took time, she took a long time, but she seemed to be getting nowhere. And she had not said a word. In the lighted room she looked like a child who had put on her father's clothes, playing grown up, and had grown tired of the game. Any moment now she would throw all those clothes around. Maybe go into tantrums.

Later Sol said, "I'm not hurrying you, but if you want to take that bus . . ."

"Oh, Sol! " Blanche cried, standing abruptly, "Don't let us go tonight. Perhaps . . . well, any time you say so." She walked towards the child and picked him up, saying, "May I . . . I mean, may we stay? "

"Jerry, look, your mom's crying."

Sol bought Jerry warm baby things. He bought Blanche dresses, underthings, frilly and soft and warm. Leather shoes, a pair of gloves, a scarf, blouses. No, no, no! she kept protesting yet she loved the new things.

"It's about time you wore something that fit. Something that makes you look what you really are, a girl. Right? "

Back in the apartment, she tried them on again, asking him, "How's this? And this? And this? Like it? " She didn't seem to know what to do, putting on one after another. At one point, Sol said, "You look like a bride."

A cloud darkened her face. She looked old, suddenly old.

"What's the matter? " Sol asked.

"I've never . . ." she faltered, choking on her words, "I've never . . . anything like these."

She rushed to him, putting her arms around him, kissing his cheek. She smelled . . . like new clothes.

"Jerry," she said, turning to the baby in his spanking new outfit, playing with plastic blocks, "Kiss Mr. Sol thanks."

In spite of his mother's prodding, Jerry refused and fought to get back to his toys. Sol kissed him instead.

Somehow, Blanche made her intentions clear. They would leave when he was ready to begin his trip. Meanwhile, she would help him, whatever she could do. The only trouble was, he wanted to do everything. The cooking, the cleaning. The only times he let her help was when he and Jerry were having fun playing together. He even wanted to change the baby's diapers himself, but Blanche would not let him. Once she allowed him to bathe Jerry.

"How did it go?" she asked as the two came out of the bathroom.

"Sensational," Sol said. "Wasn't it, Jerry boy?"

It could be Jerry thought so, too. He had become so attached to Sol that Blanche had to ask him to help her make Jerry do what she wanted him to, like eat or drink or go to sleep. Jerry obeyed him, believed in what Sol told him. One day as Sol was about to leave, Jerry cried and wouldn't stop until Sol returned to hush him in his arms. That day he did not go out alone. He took Jerry and his mother with him.

True to his word, Sol bought Blanche a suitcase. She kissed him on the cheek. Every time he had something for her when he came home from downtown, she rewarded him with a kiss. Sometimes they all went out together. Once they went to a movie. Too bad, Sol thought, there were no reruns of Robert Taylor movies. Blanche had heard about the actor, but she was not particularly interested in him.

"Where's he now?" she asked.

"He's dead," he said.

"When, what he died of?"

"Last summer. Cancer of the lungs."

"That gets 'em, don't it, too much smoking, I bet. That's what I tell Jerry's dad. I hate the stuff. I'm glad you don't smoke, Sol."

"That's no help, though," he said and would not explain.

Sol enjoyed their company. Too much, he was afraid. He had decided to leave on his vacation immediately. He had made up his mind to go to Washington first instead of what he had been planning in his mind about his itinerary. He had written his old buddies in California because he had planned, tentatively, on going to the West Coast first, return to Chicago after a swing to the East Coast, New York, Washington D.C., for very special reasons. He was not sure there would be time if he followed his original plan of going to Washington last. He had to see Barbara. Why? No reason. Or for a thousand reasons. Of course, there was the possibility that Barbara was no longer in Washington. Or she could be dead. The way she lived. Besides, she was older than he by ten years no less. No one would believe that. It was the truth and he didn't care. He was her baby dumpling, her angel, her lord, but heck, who was not that to her, even more, as he was to find out later? Sol shook his head to erase the memory.

"I've decided on going Greyhound myself," Sol told Blanche. "Thank me for going Greyhound, Jerry," he added, still shaking his head to blot out the memory.

One night he woke up to find Blanche standing near his bed in her new flimsy nightgown looking very much like the picture of "Editha and the Burglar," a story his American teachers taught him in high school in the Philippines.

"Sol! Sol! " she was crying. "What's the matter?"

"What?" he asked, pain all over his body.

"You were moaning. Are you okay, Sol?"

"I'm okay."

"Sure?"

"Sure."

She sat on the side of the bed and took his hand, pressing it lightly. Without meaning to, he held on to her tightly in gratitude. He was safe and across the river of a hundred man-eating crocodiles all in one piece, hurting a bit, but the pain would soon be gone. If he was given a last wish, it would be for someone to be around, anyone, and hold his hand when the end was near. However, from the way he was feeling, this was not yet that moment.

"Move over. Let me lie down beside you. That's better. Are you sure you're okay, Sol? Last night, you were crying; I thought I heard you. I wasn't sure. But you were like tonight."

"Jerry might fall off, looking for you," he said.

"He's okay," she said, moving closer, pressing her body to his. "Gee, it's nice in here. With you. Sure, you don't mind? You okay now, I hope."

"Sure."

She lay on her back, her hands under her head. She was staring at the ceiling.

"It ain't so dark here," she said.

"There's a street lamp outside," he said.

"It's raining again. Listen."

"I guess so."

She lay on her side facing him. "I'd say you're something, Sol. You remind me of . . ."

"Yes?" he said, turning his head to her.

"It's funny, but you remind me of a saint."

"Shit," he said.

"You're a saint. You got to be. 'cept that you're rich. Saints are poor, isn't it?"

"I don't know. But I'm not rich."

"Yes, you are."

"And I'm not a saint."

"Yes, you're, too."

She put her arms around him. "Put your arms around me, Sol. That's it. That's nice. You're not hurting now, are you?"

"No," he said, truthfully.

"But you got pains, right? I seen all those bottles. I seen you take 'em pills."

"I'm okay now." He wanted to hold her hand, but he dared not move. She was so close, he could not reach her hand without touching her thighs.

"Sol, you been married before?" she whispered, her breath warm on his face.

"No, never."

"Why not?"

"Never got around to it, I guess. Nobody wanted me enough to marry me."

"That's a laugh. I would'a married you."

"Yep. Perhaps in those days."

"Now. I mean now."

There was a constriction in his breast that was a mixture of pain and sweetness. His heart was pounding, then missed a beat or two. It was like dying and yet not like it. He was breathing hard.

"What's the matter, Sol?"

"Nothing."

"You had girls?"

"Yep."

"I thought so."

"That was years ago. Maybe, before you were born."

"Too bad."

"Too bad, what?"

"You coulda made some girl happy."

"I don't know. But something always happened."

"Like what?"

"They got tired of me before I got tired of them."

"Some girl treat you bad?"

"No. I treat 'em bad."

"I don't believe you. Why, you're the finest man I ever seen. You couldn't treat nobody bad no matter how hard you tried."

"You don't know me. You see, I was very jealous."

"Oh. That's bad."

"Yep. The girls couldn't stand me. I wanted 'em all to myself."

"That's great. I want my man to feel that way about me."

"I guess I spoiled 'em, too. With too much care. Too much everything."

"I can see that. Like I say, you're a saint."

"It's late. Better sleep now."

"I wanna stay here, Sol. Put your arm around me. There. I love you, Sol."

"Nonsense."

"Want me to go?"

"No. Stay. You keep me warm."

"I do? I thought I did nothing to you."

"Hush."

"Sol . . . I'm clean now, ain't I? Smell my hair. Like it? There. Smell that."

She cuddled deeper into his arms, her body parts filling every lack in his, her warmth flowing into him, but there was no nourishment in it, no strength. On the contrary, there was a wasting away.

"Stop moving," he breathed huskily as she kept on fitting herself into him. Slowly, at first, then fiercely, her mouth was seeking his and he couldn't breathe. She had found him at last, but she had no way of knowing and it was much too late for him to make her know. There, there, that's me.

Breaking away, he jumped off the bed and ran to the bathroom. His pajamas were soaking wet and sticky between his legs. He could feel it oozing out. Like something terrible was spilling out of him, it felt good, it felt great, he wanted to scream and applaud. This had not happened to him in years. It just came. He thought he had been drained of all that stuff. And the damn thing was as limp as ever. He removed his pajama trousers and wiped himself. It had shrivelled into a mere nothing with neither shame nor pride, a neutral observer, shit! He turned on the hot water and cleaned himself and changed into another pair of pajamas. He threw the soiled one into the hamper. As he stole quietly back to bed, he hoped she would not notice that he had different pajamas on.

"What took you so long?" she asked, adjusting the sheet over them. "Gee, you smell nice."

"Thanks. what did you expect? You thought I'd smell like a rat after . . .

She put a finger on his lips, patting his face and moving closer.

"You don't want to," she whispered.

"How do you know?"

"I can tell," she said as she buried her head in his shoulder, adding, "You smell good. You're a very clean man, you know."

He was going to say, you bet, but that would not exactly be the truth.

"You smell like a saint," she said, drowsily. "Night, saint."

They would all be leaving in a couple of days. He had convinced himself that Blanche was simply trying to pay him back out of gratitude, her way of saying, thank you for everything you've done for Jerry and me. And she could not be blamed, poor child, for trying to make payment in her own currency. It was all she could afford.

Yet it was not easy convincing himself that he really wanted to be left alone. If he were to be honest to himself, the truth was, he wanted them around. He had never felt what it was like to have a baby walking towards him, rushing into his arms, quieting down when he held him, looking up to him, crying whenever he left the apartment without them. Sometimes when this happened, he didn't feel like leaving. "Come along," he said. But Blanche knew better.

"Don't spoil him, Sol. Ignore him and go. He'll stop crying," she said.

Too late now, indeed, for a lot of things he had long forgotten or had never known. It felt good having someone to come home to, like the song said. It felt nice having someone close and warm.

"Could be this is all we need," he told her once, "A little warmth, is all."

"A little only?"

"That's enough, no? Seems that's all life is about. Too much would burn us, scald us to death."

There was no use hiding the truth from Blanche. She knew about his pains. She had heard him moaning, crying in his sleep. She had watched him, unknown to him, his face contorted in pain, unable to sleep. Knowing this now, he wished he had never known her. And for other reasons.

"What does your doctor say?" she asked him once.

"Nothing. Prescribes medicines, all pain killers, for temporary relief only. Take it easy. Don't eat this, don't eat that. I'm just old, I guess. Too old even for a complete overhauling. Final destination: junkyard."

"Quit talking like that. Do you no good."

"Well, I'm dying. That's all."

"No, you're not. You're not! " she shouted.

"Easy. What's wrong with dying? I've lived long enough, had all the time. I could have lived better. Otherwise, what else could I want?"

"Let's quit this talk, okay?"

"Okay. What shall we talk about? The moon and the stars? The green of your eyes? Say, you must be a jealous person, too. Aren't you, now?"

"What gets me is, it ain't fair. Everything I get to like, I lose, I can't hold. I always lose. A born loser, that's me."

"It can't be that bad, Blanche. Besides, you're young."

"I've just known you. It's a experience. Nice. In all my life, in all my goddamned life, nothing like it. Then it's over, finished. Like you, what you're saying now."

"So I'm gonna live forever and ever! " Sol was trying to sound very theatrical.

"I don't mean that. You know I don't. But you talk like you know when. Like when the rent's due. Or something."

"Let me put it this way, I'm getting ready. I want to be prepared. Always prepared, like a good boy scout."

"You are a educated man, I'm sure. They must have learned you some place how you know when you're gonna die. Right?"

"No school can teach you that. Nobody knows, that's the truth. But there are signs. There's a superstition we have in the islands. When a sick person begins to see his dead relatives in his dreams, that's bad."

"Baloney! I always dream of my father when I ain't well."

"I'm talking of a Philippine superstitution, not American."

"So what?"

"Besides, in the dream the visit is only a sign. Nothing happens to the sick one unless his folks—in the dream—bring him something to eat. When the sick one eats what's given him, well, that's the end of the ball game."

"Don't eat if it's that bad."

"But it's a dream, see? You can't change a dream. A dream's a dream."

"Change the superstition. I don't see why not. Things changing all the time. Men go back and forth to the moon. It's a lousy superstition."

"I believe you, Blanche, honest. But there are things that can't be changed. Or explained."

"Nonsense. I know. Mr. Sol King wanna die. He's dying to die. Nothing will stop him. Let's go, Jerry."

The day Sol left by bus for Washington, Blanche and Jerry took another bus for Dowagiac. They rode in a cab to the depot. It was a cold sunny day. In their new attire they didn't look like the same mother and child whom he had taken home with him on the night of the big snowstorm more than a week ago. Jerry sat between them in the backseat with Sol's arm around the baby's shoulder while Blanche held his arm. Her eyes were red from crying. But it was Jerry in his mind. The child had been unusually good that day. When Blanche pulled him away to keep him from getting in the way while Sol was busy packing his things, he obeyed without a struggle. He let his mother scrub him clean, put on his new green sweater and red slacks like a little gentleman as Blanche called him. Sol was thinking, this child would not remember any of these days. After a few days in Dowagiac, what would Sol be to him? Nothing. He was sure he was going to miss the child. The very first thing he wanted to see every morning when he woke up was little Jerry. Time went by so quickly while they were around, Blanche and Jerry. But it was time to go, time to put an end to what could be at best or at the worst a temporary detour.

The bus for Dowagiac was scheduled to leave an hour earlier than the bus he was taking for Washington, D.C. Sol helped them check their luggage. Blanche was almost pretty in her new red coat and tall in her medium high heeled shoes. It was obvious she was holding back her tears, trying hard to smile. Sol had asked her not to make a scene. While they were waiting in line before the passengers were called in at the gate, Sol took Jerry in his arms. When it was time to board the bus, the child would not go back to his mother. He cried and kicked, struggling against Blanche who could not move on. They were slowing down the line and creating quite the scene Sol had wanted to avoid. He had to walk with Blanche to the gate. As they passed through, Sol moved away, pushing the child into her arms where he kept struggling and screaming at the top of his voice.

Blanche hurried to the bus and got on without looking back.

Sol waited behind the glass panel, waving his hands towards the bus without seeing any sign of mother and child. Perhaps they had taken a seat on the other side, he thought, until he saw Jerry propped up by his mother against the bus window, his little fists banging away silently. Just as silent were his frantic cries that showed in his open mouth and wild eyes.

Sol turned away from the gate as the bus drove off behind a fleet of buses parked in rows, each marked with the name of the city of its destination. Sol was interested only in Washington D.C. And he still had an hour. Well, a little less, maybe.

You leave home and country, seek sanctuary in an alien land, refuge in another idiom, but you remain on the outside, you are neither called nor chosen; and you keep running, stumbling along the road over a snag of rocks, a net of thread at the feet, a clouding over in the mind, but it is only the surging forward that is momentarily checked, the motion continues, circular into nowhere; backward to what had been the native land, its warmth, its horrid climate, the farce of its form of government, the kindness of the poor, their hunger, their sentimentality; and forward again into a glut of strangeness that never becomes familiar, an embarrassment of colors, a negative in black and white blown out of proportion.

Who needs to run?

Besides, listen to that wayward heart. Look at those old, arthritic legs. How could you run?

Long before the bus had passed the skyway, Sol realized that he had chosen a bad time for travel. Yet he had to be on his way. There was not much choice left. Many of the letters he had written using the old addresses were returned unopened, marked: Address Unknown. It had been a long time.

He had travelled all over the United States as a young man in search of jobs and friends, a congenial spot, or for no reason at all, but goaded on by fate, which he believed in. Up and down the California coast, across the continent, stopping briefly for a glimpse of the sign that said stay, this is the place, and failing to see it, moved on, restless and eager to touch places with the strangest names—Goldfield, Duckwater, Castledale, Split Rock, Mayhill, Mount Cloud—or places with no names and holding no promise. Yet if fate had said stay, he would have tarried. But no, fate urged him on. The bigger, brighter cities held him longer, New York, Washington D.C., Chicago. He thought it would be Washington to the very end until that day he came running to Chicago, where he had been earlier in his younger days. Fate must have spoken as it always did in his life. Chicago became home where the years came and went. Perhaps there would be time to return. Who could tell? All he knew now, the hour was late.

Travelling by bus in winter, there was nothing much to see. He didn't know where he was and he didn't care. Half asleep, he could feel the bus slowing down as it turned round the ramp of an exit for a brief rest stop, the glare of neon lights after a passage through the dark highways touching his closed eyes, prying them open, and there were flashes of names, an eating place, a gasoline station, the price per gal. emphatic in its size, and to the ignorant alien (which he was not!), rather bewildering, a motel, the word VACANCY in bright electric coils winking obscenely.

He recalled other times to brighten the drabness of the trip. After all, he had a hoard of memories. He had seen riots, watched cities burn, men screaming in panic like hogs speared into running towards their death in their long and narrow pens, a headlong movement it always was, a jostling and squealing of fright and pain.

There were colors and smells to remember—and scenes. Colors of autumn, smell of smoke under the elms, odor of fertilizer along the farmlands in the Midwest, scent of apples and dung, rustle of dry leaves and tight coughing in the parks, birdsongs and bird-shit, children dancing in the streets, crawling at the feet of winos sleeping off their drunk in summer time, segregated beaches, restricted camps in upper Michigan, all through the fickle seasons, quickly passing like the cherry blossoms at the Tidal Basin or permanent like the snowcapped mountains in the Northwest.

He willed hard to sleep. He had a bottle of tylenol handy whenever the pain was too much to bear and sleep was impossible. He could tell—sometimes afterwards on awaking—if he had actually fallen asleep, for then there was no pain at all and the roll of the bus was a hammock swinging between two tamarind trees in the backyard of someone's childhood, maybe his. And the driver's voice over the speaker announcing Cleveland, Pittsburgh, Breezewood, died away in a baby's tinkling laugh and a voice close in his ears asking, shall we not see you again? Is this the last time? But why? Why?

Or there was a dream, a cameraman's error of a dream, the same film used twice, slides of scenes and events superimposed twice over and developed into a disconcerting montage, a weird combination of places and differing times and people out of the present and the past.

There was Luz, not the shy brown girl in the yellowing snapshot but an old peasant woman selling banana fritters at the foot of a concrete stairway leading nowhere in the shadow of the ruins

154

of war while close by Barbara stood, gray-haired and a bit stooped with the same smile that lighted up her pale, wrinkled face, obviously waiting for her change. Luz shifted the hot fritters held together with a stick, from one hand to the other. They talked soundlessly. Something must have gone wrong, an audio network trouble, but they looked friendly, each it seemed sharing with the other a long kept secret, a common hurt that didn't matter anymore.

A small child who looked very much like Jerry was toddling on the grass leading to the steps of the Jefferson Memorial and as Sol shouted for him to watch out, the child took a turn and stood on the white beach of Sorsogon, his tiny white body naked in the sun. The water lapped at his feet and he was about to cry. Sol sprinted towards him before the waves could strike him down. Jerry, Jerry, he cried, putting his arms around the child, you're cold, where are all those clothes I gave you?

A succession of clicks and a buzzing sound perhaps from an over-heated projector: Along the bridle paths in Rock Creek Park, little brown farmer boys led their carabaos to graze at will. They stared in amazement at the tall red-faced Americans walking by.

And there was Mount Mayon, its flame-tipped crater belching smoke that darkened the skies over Arlington Cemetery while a caisson draped in the Stars and Stripes rolled by, with soldiers marching to the ruffle of silent drums. It was a heavy silence except for the blurred sound of the bus engine and the wheels on the highway.

In this other scene Sol was cruising for passengers in his cab, taking in an old couple who wanted to visit the White House. The taxi reeled sidewise and as he looked out to check for a possible flat tire, he noticed that he was passing through the cobblestone roads of Binondo in Manila. There was that pain again and he gripped the wheel, bending close to it. As he raised his head for air, he saw through the rear view mirror the old couple in the back seat, clasped in each other's arms, their cheeks pressed together, their eyes closed, their faces radiant with something like love or ecstasy. They were his parents. *"Inang, Tatang,"* he cried, turning to them. The couple stirred. No, they were not his parents. They were the same old American tourists who wanted to see the White House.

The taxi rolled round and round past the Circles with the mounted men. There was not a soul in sight. Where have all the other tourists gone? A woman's voice was crooning, good night, wherever you are . . . Sol turned off the radio. Here we are, folks.

But the couple had gone back to sleep. How cold they looked. Sol removed his parka and placed it over them. As he stared at their faces, he realized they were dead. Mr. Swingle must have worked hard at them. Like they were only fast asleep. Now what was he to do? He glanced towards the White House and for the first time he noticed the barbed wire around it, familiar like the board now swinging in the wind with the words in black paint that still looked wet: OFF LIMITS, NO TRESPASSING, U.S. PROPERTY.

𝒱

As soon as he arrived in Washington D.C., he spent a great deal of his time leafing through the telephone directory, looking for the names of those he knew way back in the forties. There were not too many anymore. What did he expect? The way of the exile was a series of passing through, a habit of roads, and the highways were so easy and inviting.

"Most of 'em are dead now," Noli said, comfortable in his wheelchair, his gray hair like a touch of winter, part of the slush and snow that covered the ground all the way from Washington D.C. to his neat cottage in Lanham, Maryland. He was among the first Sol tried to get in touch with as soon as he reached Washington and he was glad he had succeeded. Both of them were happy to see each other.

About thirty years ago, Sol and Noli roomed in an apartment on Fourth and F Street N.W., a few blocks from Benny's Barbershop where they passed the time with other Filipinos on weekends or when they had nothing to do nights and wanted company. They heard all the news about Filipinos in Washington, D.C. in the barbershop. They played knock rummy, checkers, or sat around watching others play and banter with one another, their voices high-pitched and loud and jolly as they had to compete with the radio that was on all the time the barbershop was open for business.

The black Cadillac alongside the street near the main entrance was evidence that business was good. Benny became an object of ill-concealed envy among his friends and customers, both Filipinos and Americans, and the butt of jokes because of that car. They relished kidding him about it. Some said that it was not really his, that it belonged to a funeral home, which had to park it some place and Benny was getting paid for taking care of it. Others said that he moonlighted as agent for the funeral home. Besides, it was a fantastic conversation piece, a decoy to attract more customers. The truth was that it was really his. He didn't need any more than the customers he had. As it was, he worked twelve, fourteen hours a day. He lived in the shop, practically. Taking another barber was out of the question. Customers came for Benny only.

The barbershop remained open even when he was not around. When that happened, he was sure to be elsewhere, most likely in the home of the Philippine Resident Commissioner, cutting his hair. When customers came, that was what they were told by the Filipinos in the barbershop. Once, President Quezon himself sent for him to cut his hair at his suite in the Shoreham Hotel. After that, Benny's fortune was made. Soon after, the Cadillac became a familiar sight on the street corner. Yet Benny made no attempt to buy new equipment, the worn out appearance of the shop becoming, as it were, part of the attraction of Benny's Barbershop. Besides, he would say, this is a one-man barbershop, and this man's "da best."

For much more than this, many Filipinos, including those who lived in the suburbs, spent much of their free time with Benny, listening to the news and the gossip, contributing their own to the melange of fact and fiction. For many of them this was the only place where they could laugh and hear laughter without anybody screaming at them to shut up. Nobody minded the noise, the babel of tongues in many dialects with English seemingly just one of them. In the war years, before and after, Benny's had become a central news agency of sorts for Filipinos and their American friends.

It was here that Sol learned of a yo-yo contest sponsored by the local Rexall Drugstore. The prize was a job promoting the sales of the well-known Duncan Yo-Yo. At that time, Noli was looking for a job. Although he was not too good at it, Noli had impressed

158

Sol with his routine. So he wasted no time telling Noli about the contest.

Most of the contestants were Filipinos, all of them perhaps were, except that some did not look like Filipinos. Mestizos perhaps. They were tall with high bridged noses and fair complexioned. And they were good, all of them. Noli appeared inept, a novice in their midst, and he was the shortest, a pygmy among giants. The fact of his size alone was sufficient to discourage Noli. But he needed the job. Sol encouraged him. Remember David and Goliath? Or just think you are a dime among nickels, ha, ha!

The two friends watched the others go through their paces while they waited for the contest to begin. From the look in his face, Noli was certain he had no chance. They could spin the top with both hands better than Noli could with one hand, which was easier. Noli could work out with both hands, too, he knew how to do most of the trick patterns, the loop-the-loops, over-the-falls, which Filipinos called *Hinulugang Taktak*, elevators, the rattat-tat or machine-guns, the meow or skin-the-cat, but he missed quite often, abominably.

Sol acted as his second, his manager, his morale booster. Long before the preliminaries were over, Sol knew his man was not in their class. He would not make it. But he continued to cheer him up. The contestants worked out in groups. Every time Noli looked his way, Sol cheered him up with a gesture and an encouraging word and Noli's teeth showed in a smile on his sweat-soaked face.

Many of the other contestants breezed through the basics, the "sleeping," "walking the dog," and "rock the cradle." By the time he was ready for the last routine, Noli was sweating so much with the effort, Sol wanted to stop the torture and ask him to drop out of the contest. There was no use. The others were so good, it would be difficult choosing from among them.

As Noli was flexing his fingers, rubbing the sore spots, before attempting the "rock the cradle," the Chairman of the Board of Judges, representatives of the Duncan Yo-Yo Company and the manager of the Rexall Drugstore at the Dupont Circle where the contest was being held, stood on a bench and announced the finalists. Noli was among them.

Sol jumped with delight, waving his arms, dancing about, and stopped only when the man asked for silence as he proceeded to announce details of the finals. It was a make or break "loop-the-loops" marathon. With one mistake, the contestant was out. Eliminated. Each contestant had to perform individually. Until then the contestants worked out simultaneously in groups. One name was called.

A tall young man with bushy eyebrows stood on a bench and began the routine. His yo-yo was a flashy Duncan Imperial, each half spangled with bright stones of many colors. As he spun it around, there was a riot of whirling stars. The crowd that filled the entire area of the Circle facing the drugstore stood in wonder, as their eyes followed those stars falling all around them. Poor Noli and his cheap toy!

There was a time limit. Some committed mistakes out of sheer nervousness before they got going. Always, each spun around a top of dazzling beauty.

Noli was the last to be called. He was so short that the people at the rear had to crane their necks to see him. Some must have thought he was not standing on the bench like the others. His yo-yo was a colorless toy little boys played with in their backyard, on the stoop of the stairs, on their summer porches. Sol could not bear the sight of Noli, waiting for the signal to begin. His friend looked so small, so pitiful if he wasn't so funny in his oversized suit. Sol looked away. But before he could look again, the contest was over. One of the judges walked towards Noli, practically lifting him from the bench as he raised Noli's hand in victory.

Sol didn't know what had happened. From the look on Noli's face, he didn't seem to know either. As winner, he should be smiling and happy, but it seemed he was going to cry. The crowd was in an uproar. There was a lot of protesting from the other contestants and their friends, loud, harsh words, but the judges had spoken. Their judgment was final. They made the rules as the contest went along and interpreted them as they wished.

When Sol finally got to his side, he said, "You've won. You've won, Noli. Cheer up." But the little man still looked dazed. His fingers hurt, he wanted to cry. Perhaps he was crying except that his face was wet all over with sweat, it was hard to tell.

Noli's main qualification was his height or his lack of height. The job called for a short man, the shorter the better. Just why the contest rules did not specify this particular requirement had never been clear. Perhaps no one thought of it until they saw Noli among those tall men. And it was easy enough. It didn't call for an expert yo-yo player, much less a champion. He could make as many mistakes as would be inevitable in Noli's case. What was needed was stamina to stand on his feet, spinning the yo-yo any routine he felt like doing, five hours a day with fifteen minutes break between hours and the usual hour free for lunch.

Sol brought him his lunch. He worked near the drugstore in a printing shop, carting away finished posters and cleaning the premises at closing time. His work did not begin until one in the afternoon so he had ample time to prepare a hot lunch for both of them. They ate on the grass in the shade of a tree. It was a hot summer.

Once while they were eating, Sol asked to see his hands, but Noli kept them behind him. Sol noticed that some of his fingers were purple, almost livid. He had asked him to use gloves, but Noli said he couldn't spin the yoyo well with gloves on.

The first time Sol mingled with the crowd that daily watched Noli performing inside the show window of the drugstore, he felt bad. He blamed himself for getting him into it. There was the usual crowd of pedestrians gawking in front of the show window, which was decorated with the familiar designs of the yo-yo Duncan Industries manufactured. Apart from these, it was bare. Noli stood in the middle on stockinged feet, dressed in a pleated dark blue zoot suit, which made him look even shorter. He was sweating profusely in spite of two small electric fans beamed on him, as he spun a red, white, and blue yoyo, making the usual mistakes, which went over big with the children in the audience, who asked for more. Noli was acting like a clown, a monkey. There was pain in the little fellow's eyes Sol could not bear to see.

"Get another job," Sol told him once.

"The pay's good," Noli said.

"It's so good, you could afford a grand funeral."

"It's not bad. My hands will soon get callouses and that would be fine. No more pain then."

"You'll have no fingers before you get callouses."

"I'll be all right," Noli insisted.

Sometimes, when Sol came home late at night from work, he would find Noli putting salve on his wounds.

After a month, Noli quit for a different reason, wounded pride. He could no longer take the ribbing at the barbershop.

"I really felt like a monkey," he confided to Sol, "and I was afraid I was beginning to look like one and thinking like one. One day I saw some children carrying small paper bags and I thought they were going to feed me peanuts. I was getting crazy. Perhaps I was, already."

When the war came, most of the Filipinos volunteered and were taken into the U.S. Army. Sol was 4-F as he had a job by then with an ammunition factory. Noli was turned down because of his height. He was shorter than the rifle they gave him, the joke went around. The two friends drifted from one job to another, and somehow lost track of each other.

Sol did not know Noli had married. What did he expect? Even little guys had their own little women. To each his own. Except that his wife was not little. The butt of jokes all his life, Noli once again invited ridicule by marrying a Philippine girl who towered over him. She had come to Washington as a maid for one of the clerks in the Philippine Resident Commissioner's Office. She was thin like a toothpick and plain with scraggly hair that was almost always white with dandruff. Her buck teeth and a pug nose over distended nostrils made her look like a cartoon character. Her eyes were mere slits and completely disappeared when she smiled, but then nobody missed them.

"Remember Ruth?" Noli said as his wife joined them. She was now matronly stout, all buck teeth gone, replaced by life-like dentures, a different nose, pert and smallish, her hair, doubtless a wig, was light brown, touched with slivers of gray and completely dandruff free.

"No!" Sol exclaimed. He was immediately sorry for showing surprise, but he couldn't help it. He had known the other Ruth, not this one.

"She takes care of me," Noli said. "I'd be in a home now without her."

Ruth smiled a young pretty smile.

"This house is ours," she said. "It has been paid for. Noli earns enough. I don't have to work."

Sol could not hide the perplexity in his face. Why did she have to give all that information? It sounded like boasting. Noli must have been embarrassed himself. He raised the one hand he could move, reaching over his shoulder to touch Ruth's hand, which rested on the back of the wheel chair.

The truth was Noli was hard working. He didn't have a vice, major or minor, as the joke among Filipinos went, and he saved some. Shortly after his retirement, he supplemented his pension working at odd jobs until he had the stroke.

"I drove a minibus for a home, collecting the aged and delivering 'em to churches Sundays and bringing 'em back. Some were younger than me. Not a one of 'em was Filipino. Pinoys scared of homes. Like they're scared of hospitals. They prefer to die in their rooms. Have you seen those rooms in cheap rundown buildings? Jeesus!"

"Noli's very good. He look after the old guys who're alone,"

Ruth said, passing her hand lightly on Noli's head.

"Hell, I was luckier than them," Noli said and paused. "Until that damn stroke felled me." Another pause. "Hell, even now I'm luckier than the alone ones. I got Ruth here, see?"

Ruth's hand on his head became a caress, her fingers playing on the back of his neck. Noli seemed to love it.

"But, hell, they didn't want no care. So long they got some dough, they never mind nothing."

"He's right," Ruth said, applauding from the gallery.

"Hope you saved enough yourself, Sol. You can never have too much dough in this country. As we always say, it's a free country where everything's paid for."

"I got enough for . . . for . . . I got enough, sure."

"Glad to hear that. You see, other o.t.'s don't have common sense. It's gamble, gamble all the time. They got to do something, see? They should've married their favorite whores."

"I know some who did," Ruth said.

"Yep. Hell, it's no way to live. You seen some of 'em, Sol."

Yes, indeed. The old brown rags of men wandering the streets in all the cities he had been, loitering in bus depots, crowding in cheap hotel lobbies in front of TV sets, watching whatever was on to pass the time. They walked the streets in all weathers, looking into the eyes of all brown men who could be Filipino, trying to strike up a conversation, hurrying after them inside men's rooms to exchange a few words in the dialect, slowly realizing but refusing to admit that nobody, least of all their own countrymen, wanted to have anything to do with them. Those who were too old and too weak to go outdoors stayed in their rooms all day, sleeping or doing nothing at all. They listened for footsteps in the corridors or sounds of alarm or rain out in the streets, the ring of the telephone if they kept one. Those who had TV watched all day and were grateful for the sound of voices and singing and laughter in their final room. In the silence, alone too long, you begin to talk to yourself. The first time you hear the sound of your own voice, you panic. Sol knew.

"I guess they need the excitement, that's why they gamble. When they win, they forget all past losses and they celebrate by gambling again and losing."

"That's all excites 'em now," Ruth said.

"You can say that again, sweetheart. But, hell, when they're broke they do all sorts of things. You've seen 'em walking from phone booth to another, sticking their finger into the coin slot that's empty anyhow."

"Least they don't steal. Beg maybe," Ruth said. She seemed to know a lot about them.

"They're too scared to do that. It's scary enough to be old and helpless in this country, you know that." Noli was addressing both of them.

"Must be terrible. Nothing to do. And alone. Just waiting to die," Ruth said in a tone as casual as telling the two old friends that dinner would be a little late. Sol squirmed but tried hard not to show it. Noli appeared as if he had not heard. It was possible, too, that he no longer listened to her.

"Some lose their minds. You knew Bart, didn't you? Bartolomeo Despi or something," Noli said.

"Yes, yes," Sol answered quickly. Bart was the guy who always held a cap folded in his hand. He had never seen him wearing it, but he seemed lost without it in his hand, a crumpled piece of dirty rag. "I know him. He had the most dangerous job during the war, hauling T.N.T. My job was easy as pie compared to his. Why, every night we waited for him in the Manila House on Columbia Road and until we saw him in his usual corner we were afraid he wasn't going to show up."

"He survived all right. But he's nuts now. They took him away. His basement room was smelly as hell. He was making bombs he says, all sorts of equipment in there like he was really making bombs and he was not kidding, 'cept he used face powder or something like starch instead of the real stuff. He says he's making 'em bombs to drop on the oppressors of our country."

"What oppressors?" Sol asked.

"He didn't say. He made speeches against tyrants, his loud voice disturbing the neighborhood. They took him away in a panel truck."

"Whatever happened to Benny? The barbershop's still there?"

"Nah! Gone a long time ago. It's now a eating place, soul food. Benny just drove away one day in his Cadillac, a new model, believe me. Never heard of him again."

"Must be parked somewhere if he's still alive," Ruth said, walking out of the room.

"You know Pete, the guy who's nuts on physical culture? He wants to be another Atlas and beginning to look like one. Well, he die last year."

"Broke a blood vessel lifting those weights?"

"Nah! He swallow a fishbone in his windpipe," Noli said, looking around to be sure they were alone. "Sol, I know who you want to see. Barbara," he added, in a voice so soft, Sol barely heard him.

"Where's she? Do you know?"

"Have you tried her old place, your old place in the north-west, Belmont, ain't it?"

"She doesn't live there anymore."

"I'll be darned. Try the homes. The better ones. She loves comfort. If she's still here, she won't be living in a crummy home."

"I've looked and looked. The whole telephone directory."

"She got to be here. No other place for her. And I'm sure as hell she ain't dead. We'd have known. All the Pinoys loved her."

And she loved them all, Sol was about to say, but there was no point, no sense to that.

As they went over the listings of homes in the yellow pages, Noli looked up and asked, "Hey, Sol, what the hell for you want to see her?"

"Let's keep looking," Sol said. Perhaps there was no sense to that either, he was thinking.

$\mathcal{U}$

Sol had never been to this particular suburb of Washington. It must have been a wilderness before or farmland. The bus he took serviced the home daily, weekends included. It made a detour from its usual route and was scheduled to arrive a few minutes before the doors of the home were open to the public and two hours later, another ten or fifteen minutes before closing time for visitors on its return trip to Washington. For most of the way there was very little traffic. The parking areas around the shopping malls they passed were nearly empty. It was past noon, a sunny day, but the temperature was below freezing.

Every time he thought of Barbara— and he was thinking of her now—he often asked himself: and what about the others, the linking of lives without an actual bond, the way people could be close without their bodies actually touching, the lately adored, those despised or loved too late, worshipped and betrayed? Sometimes you were lucky you never saw them again.

He was not interested in this kind of luck. There was no timidity or fear in these remaining days. God, if only he could be sure as sometimes he was of the secret truth he held, he didn't have to worry how he could come out with it in a word or in a gesture that gave a hint of hope, of forgiveness for all who needed absolution before death and, also, of compassion.

The bus had slowed down rounding an exit ramp into a two-way road and after two red lights, it rolled easier down a country highway. The home was the only building for miles around, an expanse of snow-flecked development area. A driveway led into what looked like a vast playground which in other seasons must have been grassland. He could imagine the infirm among the old folks living here being wheeled around by prim uniformed attendants. Some would be walking or sitting down when they grew weary. Those bare trees with their leafy branches would afford them cool shade. The surrounding landscape had the proud look of a country club where he had worked, except that there were no tennis courts, no mini-golf courses and swimming pools. A frozen fountain and a birdbath stood near a side gate below the windows of an unfinished wing of the complex.

The lobby was crowded with visitors and noisy with their chatter. Most of them had come on the same bus. Soft music crept in from nowhere like necessary background to the incessant talk, the laughter, the smiles, the eyes touching everything. Beyond, on either side of the information counter, were other rooms just as spacious and clean. Everything appeared to have been designed for both comfort and safety. Silver handlebars lined most of the walls, looking more decorative than functional. The entire floor area was level. A wheel chair could roll through it without impediment. Brown and green rugs carpeted the floor from wall to wall. At a glance, he saw no less than two color TV sets, both of them on, although there was only an old lady sitting in front of one of them.

He had talked to Barbara on the phone. There was a long wait and a lot of interference before she could get on the line. He was nervous but tried not to show it. Noli and Ruth were watching him very closely.

"It's the switchboard girl. She must have sent someone to look for her."

"If she's not in her room, she must be strong enough to walk," Noli said.

"Even if she isn't, she won't stay in her room all day long," Ruth said.

"At least, she's well," Sol said. He removed his hand from the mouthpiece, saying with his eyes and head, she's coming. Swallowing hard, he spoke into the phone, "Hello . . . " his voice no louder than a whisper.

There was sudden static in the earphone that hurt his ear. He moved it away involuntarily. As he put it back close enough not to miss a word, he heard more static, clicks and tinny sounds, a whispering in the background. The switchboard girl must be new in her job. The static persisted but gradually faded as the whispering in the background became clearer. There were several voices saying the same lines as in a chorus, all women voices, vaguely familiar as were the words they said: "What spell have you cast on me? When will the spell be broken?" And a voice so much like his own it could have been his, indeed, rose above the chorus, silencing the speakers. "There, the spell is broken at last. You're free. See the prince turned into a frog. The royal rose garden—I never promised you one, no, no!—into a swamp alive with the croaking of frogs and the voice of the turtle. The royal palace, into a bus depot. You're free, free!"

Then it was Barbara speaking on the line. That was her voice.

"It's Barbara!" Sol said excitedly, turning to the couple, who had waited until they were certain he had succeeded in getting her on the phone. The wheel chair rolled away from him towards the outer room. But it was Noli who was pushing the chair where Ruth sat, the Ruth he knew, her buck teeth showing in a grimace of disgust as she turned to look at Sol, the dandruff falling all around her like talcum powder, but some so big they were like scales from a healed wound.

When Barbara finally knew and by the voice recognized who it was, she kept saying, "I can't believe it, can it be true, it's Sol, it's you." By the tone of her voice, she was more composed than Sol whose agitation showed not only in his difficulty with his ears and eyes, but in the utter senselessness of what he was saying. He could not remember what. Barbara understood him, however. It was she who suggested the bus. She said she would be waiting in the lobby.

Sol waited. He carried a small bundle, a light weight woolen blanket in plain green. Some time earlier as he walked around Washington, visiting familiar places, he glanced at the show windows in the business district for something appropriate to bring her. But what was appropriate? Just then it was not a matter of propriety, much less an empty gesture. He really wanted something good and useful for her. Not a peace offering. The thought embarrassed him. Could he still be holding grudges? Yet the mere fact that he was visiting her should dispel any doubt that he could still be bitter. How many times in his enforced aloneness had he said, "I have forgiven you, Barbara, you must

168

forgive me, too."

The woman approaching in his direction walked in short, slow steps, the hands on her sides hardly moving. Her hair was completely white. She was looking straight at him. In his mind, he had pictured Barbara, who was much older than he, as a gray-haired, flabby woman, as old as more than seventy years could make of the human body, but, God, not this old.

"Barbara," he said, advancing towards her.

She seemed shaken as she stood holding on to him. She felt like a load. He held on to her for fear she would fall in a heap at his feet. What could he do then, spread the blanket over her? There was something awfully wrong with the picture, a mix-up in the role each usually played.

"Sol," she said softly, her voice trembling a little, "I hardly recognized you."

He led her to the nearest chair close to a babbling group that must have comprised no less than three generations from the baby crawling on the rug while big sister was holding on to its dress, to the ancient lady sitting in the middle of moving arms and many faces.

"No, not here," Barbara said, pointing towards an inner room.

As they walked towards it with Sol supporting her, his heart beat wildly under the strain of her weight and a remembered time when the same phrase meant passion, impatient as well as illicit.

There was a love seat in the room. As they sat down, Barbara said, "You haven't changed. Now that I can see you better. Not much anyhow. I know I have."

"I have changed. Both of us. You and me . . . "

"I knew you were coming."

"Of course, you did. I talked to you on the phone."

"I don't mean that. But I knew."

"How? Who else could know? I didn't even know myself until the last hour when I decided to come."

"I knew you were coming," she insisted.

"If you say so."

"You better believe it."

"So I believe it."

"You say that like you don't. You don't believe me."

"But I do."

If they kept this way . . . but perhaps it was all they had to say to each other.

"It has been a long time."

"How have you been?"

"Fine. Everything considered. And you?"

"I'm all right, thank you."

They were repeating themselves, stealing each other's lines and still making sense. If they kept it up, they might yet find, hopefully, each other's true identity.

"Where have you been all these years?"

"Here and there. Living . . . "

"Living it up, eh?"

"No. Just living. Trying to survive."

"The same old Solomon King. Tragic sounding all the time. I bet you're loaded now. I've never seen a guy count his pennies the way you did."

Is that all you remember, was what he was going to say, but instead, he said, "I didn't want to starve. I had to make sure I didn't live on you. And I wanted to give you a lot."

Her voice was softer now as she said, "I know you did, Sol. I was just kidding."

"It's the truth, though. Besides, I didn't want to be a pauper like some of my buddies then."

"I've been here two years. I've lost touch with . . . friends."

"I had a hard time finding you."

"Why did you come?"

"I'm not sure why. Just wanted to see you, I guess. To hold your hand, maybe."

"You loved to hold hands. You really did."

"It's a nice feeling."

"Oh, Sol," she said, visibly touched, as she reached for his hand. "I knew it was you the moment I heard you."

"You remember my voice."

"Yes. And you're the only one who calls me the way you do."

"Barbara."

"Like a song. Something . . . I can't ever say it the way you do."

They looked at each other for a while. Her hand felt warm in his and, later, heavy. He wanted to put it down.

"I brought you something," he said, releasing her hand gently as he stooped to get the bundle. He placed it on her lap and watched her open it. When she saw what it was, she clasped it to her breast, saying, "It's lovely, look, how soft. Thank you, Sol."

"I'm glad you like it. It will keep you warm."

"And it's from you. Oh, Sol, I'm glad you came. It's been so long."

"I really came to Washington just to see you."

"What for, Sol?"

"Who knows what for?"

"That's right. How long are you staying?"

"I'm just passing through, really. Now that I've seen you ... "

"Where you going?"

"I don't know. I'll just keep moving, I guess."

"Aren't you passing this way again? You could, you know."

"I'm afraid not."

"I still can't believe it, you're here. I can touch you."

"I'm glad I came."

"I've often thought of you."

"Kindly, I hope."

"Sometimes."

Then there was nothing more to say. Again they were repeating themselves. She looked tired. He was not feeling too well himself. The room was over-heated. He felt pin pricks under his collar.

At her suggestion, they stood up and walked about. They had not gone far when a gentle voice came over the loudspeaker reminding everybody that visiting time would soon be over.

"You have a nice place," Sol said.

"I like it."

She pointed to the facilities of the home, which he might have overlooked, but he had seen them all or most of them. Anyhow, he was not really that interested. He could not understand what had come over him. A lightheadedness. The heat was stifling. But he was not wearing his coat. He was feverish. If he held her hand now, she would notice it.

They had reached the door, moving cautiously to the side away from the stream of people rushing to the main door. As soon as he had put on his coat, he said, "Well, Barbara, I really came to say goodbye."

"You did that years ago."

"No, I didn't. I just left. I didn't have a chance."

Every time the double doors opened and closed, Sol stood in front of her to shield her from the draft, which, somehow, refreshed him.

"Go back to your room now," he said as he let go her hand. "And don't you forget the blanket." She had left it on the seat.

Barbara took a step closer and embraced him, her gray head on his shoulder. He was so taken by surprise that they nearly fell together, but he managed to keep on his feet as he held her close. Gently, almost clumsily, he kissed her hair.

"Bye now, Barbara," he whispered.

"Bye, Sol," she said, breaking away.

As he turned to go, she waved to him, saying, "Be sure you don't catch your death out in that cold."

"Sure," he said, buttoning his coat. "Take care," he added as he fumbled for his gloves and walked through the swinging door.

The fresh air was a welcome embrace. It felt so good, he took time inhaling all that sweetness. Other visitors were getting on the bus, parked on the driveway. There was no hurry. He wanted to unbutton his coat and fill every pore of his body with that refreshing salve that now drenched his face like impalpable snow. Reluctantly, he got on the bus.

He took a seat near the window and peered outside. Not a thing to see except a blur of white and specks of black, more like shadows, here and there. It didn't feel too warm, just right. But he could hear a pounding in his breast. As he waited for it to pass, reclining on the high-backed seat, he unbuttoned his coat and removed his gloves. He closed his eyes and relaxed.

The other passengers must have been as tired as he. Everybody was quiet as the bus started smoothly. He felt it make a turn, then roll straight uphill. When he opened his eyes he thought he saw, through the windshield out in front, a broad level of sky bend down to meet them. Then he smelled a scent on his sleeves, on his hands; wherever he turned, it filled the bus. Without a doubt, it was Barbara's, a clean, antiseptic odor, pervasive, but neither happy nor sad, neutral unlike Blue Grass.

ther NEW DAY Literary Titles

Wherever he stayed for the night, there were b
ears filled with their clanging like Poe's bells for
could not tell whether they were real or part of the

From their unmarked graves, his long dead pa
and now walked the earth again, straight to his do
to their touch, his father brandishing wooden clut

"Son," his father said, giving him the clubs, "]
these to you, but I had no time. You could have
gentlest way. Here, take them. I see there are othe
flesh. And, look, I brought your mother along. Sh
for you, too."

As soon as his mother came close to him, be
bed, Sol smelled at once the lime in her hair, the cl
in her breath. She smiled sweetly as she offered h

"From Luz," she said as he reached out to
you. She has been keeping it since liberation wher
it to her. She asked me to give it to you, saying,
way.' Those were her exact words."

ENRIQUEZ, Mig Alvarez. *Three Philippine Epic Plays*

ESPINO, Federico Licsi, Jr. *Geometries Bright and Dark*

GUERRERO, Wilfrido Ma. *My Favorite 11 Plays*

JOSE, F. Sionil. *My Brother, My Executioner*
Two Filipino Women

LANOT, Marra PL. *Passion and Compassion* (Poems)

LIM, Paul Stephen. *Some Arrivals, But Mostly Departures*

MAAYO, Geraldine. *The Photographs and Other Stories*

MONTANO, Severino. *Selected Plays* (3 vols.)

MOORE, Lina Espina. *Heart of the Lotus*
A Lion in the House

MORANTTE, P.C. *God Is in the Heart* (Essays)

NORIEGA, Bienvenido. *Pares-pares* (Plays)

PERALTA, Federico. *Love Poems*

REUTER, Fr. James B. *Plays for Children*

REYES, Jun Cruz. *Utos ng Hari at Iba Pang Kuwento*

RODRIGUEZ, Nadine L. *Start of Infinity* (Poems)

SAN JUAN, E.P., Jr. *Ang mga Mangwawasak*

SANTOS, Bienvenido N. *The Praying Man*

TIEMPO, Edilberto K. *Cracked Mirror* (In process)
Finalities (Short stories)
More than Conquerors
To Be Free

TIEMPO, Edith L. *His Native Coast*

TIEMPO-TORREVILLAS, Rowena. *Upon the Willows and Other Stories*

****

Please check with your favorite bookstore in Metro Manila for the above titles, or contact NEW DAY PUBLISHERS (P.O. Box 1167, Quezon City 1100, or Tel. 928-8046; 927-5982). Subscriptions to the UPPER ROOM (English, Cebuano, Tagalog, Ilocano editions available) also accepted.

In the United States, the official distributor for NEW DAY books is: The CELLAR BOOK SHOP, 18090 Wyoming St., Detroit, Michigan 48221.